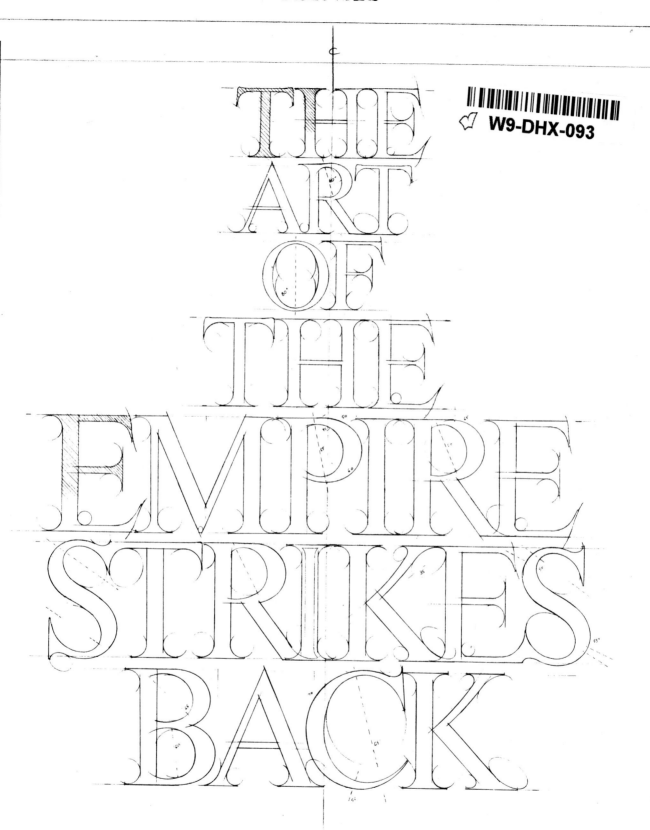

ACKNOWLEDGMENTS:

WE WOULD LIKE TO
EXPRESS THANKS TO
THOSE WHO ASSISTED IN
THE PREPARATION OF
THIS BOOK:

RITA BOZYK

MIKI HERMAN

RISA KESSLER

ELLEN KNABLE

GARY KURTZ

BARBARA LAKIN

BARRY LARIT

MELANIE PAYKOS

LARRY ROTHSTEIN

LINDSAY SMITH

KATHY WIPPERT

A DEL REY® BOOK
PUBLISHED BY BALLANTINE BOOKS

ORIGINALLY PUBLISHED IN SOMEWHAT DIFFERENT FORM BY
BALLANTINE BOOKS IN 1980.

HTTP://WWW.RANDOMHOUSE.COM/DELREY/

LIBRARY OF CONGRESS CATALOG CARD NUMBER: 96-95202

ISBN: 0-345-41088-2

COVER DESIGN BY MICHAELIS/CARPELIS DESIGN ASSOCIATES
COVER ILLUSTRATION BY RALPH MCQUARRIE

MANUFACTURED IN THE UNITED STATES OF AMERICA

FIRST EDITION: OCTOBER 1980
FIRST REVISED EDITION: FEBRUARY 1997

10 9 8 7 6 5 4 3 2 1

THE ART OF THE EMPIRE STRIKES BACK ™

TEXT BY
VIC BULLUCK AND VALERIE HOFFMAN

EDITED BY
DEBORAH CALL

ART DIRECTION AND DESIGN
VIGON, NAHAS, VIGON

A DEL REY® BOOK
BALLANTINE BOOKS · NEW YORK

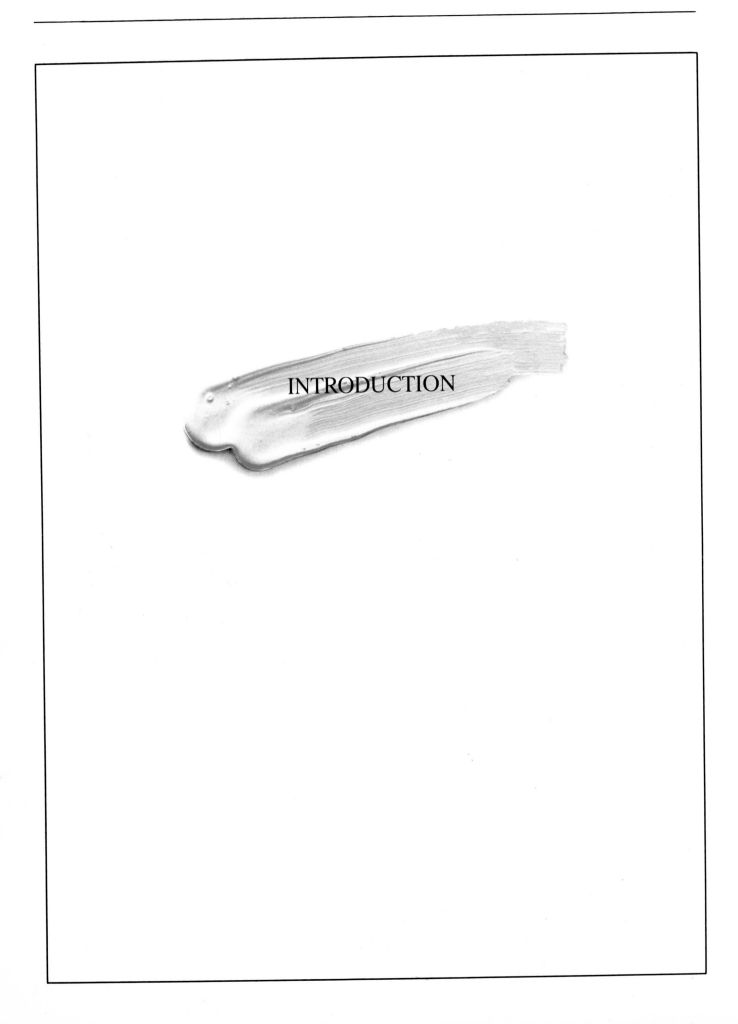

INTRODUCTION

t is not surprising to find filmgoers intensely arguing the merits of an actor, director, editor or cameraman of a film but even the most sophisticated audiences are not aware of the immense cinematic contribution made by artists and designers. They are the link between the script and the film technicians who transform the storyteller's imagination into reality.

As early as November of 1977, when a rough draft of THE EMPIRE STRIKES BACK was finished, Ralph McQuarrie and Joe Johnston began working on rough sketches for the new vehicles and characters that would appear in the film. Their work continued into the production of the film and they were joined at ILM by Johnston's assistant, Nilo Rodis-Jamero. George Lucas established ILM in Marin County to insure a home base for the technical high quality he demands in his films. It has since become a work haven for some of America's best young special effects personnel.

When the designs were fairly well established, McQuarrie began thumbnail sketches in which he played with various angles for viewing the central elements on screen. These sketches were preliminary to his production paintings which depict key scenes from the script. These paintings were used primarily to aid the production crew in the building of models, sets and costumes. They became a general reference point for everyone involved in the making of THE EMPIRE STRIKES BACK for the paintings helped to establish the mood of the film.

Simultaneously, Joe Johnston and Nilo Rodis-Jamero began to outline the action of the film in a series of detailed storyboard sketches, framed in the ratio by which the film was to be shot.

Whenever there was either a change in the script or a scene involving a special effects shot that didn't work, Johnston and Rodis-Jamero would sketch a new storyboard. Sometimes they redrew whole sequences. Most of the walls of Joe and Nilo's room at ILM are covered with storyboards. "These are only half the boards," Johnston smiled. "We just haven't put the other half up yet. When we do they'll go around the other side of the room and cover all the walls. And these boards just represent the work done involving models, matte paintings, or visual effects."

Only part of THE EMPIRE STRIKES BACK was done at ILM. A large number of storyboards were also drawn to guide the camera work of the live-action sequences that were filmed at EMI Elstree Studios in England. These storyboards were sketched by Ivor Beddoes.

The storyboards and production paintings were then given to the production designer. Although these gave him the scale and general look of the different sets, more detailing was required before each set could be built. This often meant that for practical reasons, changes in the original concept were necessary. It was the job of production designer, Norman Reynolds, to create functional stages for the actors, and design sets discussed or referred to in the script that had not been included in the production paintings. Reynolds also created all of the details which individually might have gone unnoticed but were necessary to achieve a realistic effect in the settings.

So, too, with costumes. John Mollo, costume designer, elaborated on the various sketches and paintings prepared in California, and made the actors' clothing and accessories functional.

The unique job of building the special alien creatures was handled by Stuart Freeborn. Most of his time was devoted to Yoda, the Tauntaun, the Ice Creature and revitalizing Chewbacca. Phil Tippett sculpted the clay miniatures of the Tauntaun which were used by Freeborn as a guide for the full size version. Fellow stop-motion animator, Jon Berg, worked extensively on the inner workings of the Empire's All Terrain Armored Transport.

In live action or miniatures, the final look of many scenes in THE EMPIRE STRIKES BACK depended upon the matte painters. Very early in production, decisions were made as to which sets could be built practically and which settings would be created in part or in whole with matte paintings. Harrison Ellenshaw, Ralph McQuarrie and Mike Pangrazio used the production paintings, storyboards and live action as a guide in their work to decide what portion of the frame would be matted, and then painted on a piece of glass to create the desired illusion.

Many production elements went into the making of THE EMPIRE STRIKES BACK. An inter-continental effort, it required the working cooperation of hundreds of people. This brief summary of the role of the artist understates the complexity of their interdependence as well as their constant communication with all involved with the production. Artists were essential to the creation of THE EMPIRE STRIKES BACK.

Director Irvin Kershner commented on the artists' contribution to the making of THE EMPIRE STRIKES BACK: "My concern in directing a picture is in telling a story and making the characters work within that context. In turn, the artists translate ideas into reality. They not only help make a vague idea concrete but they also bring color and texture to the film in the same way that a director brings life to it. All of these elements combine until elegance and drama are achieved."

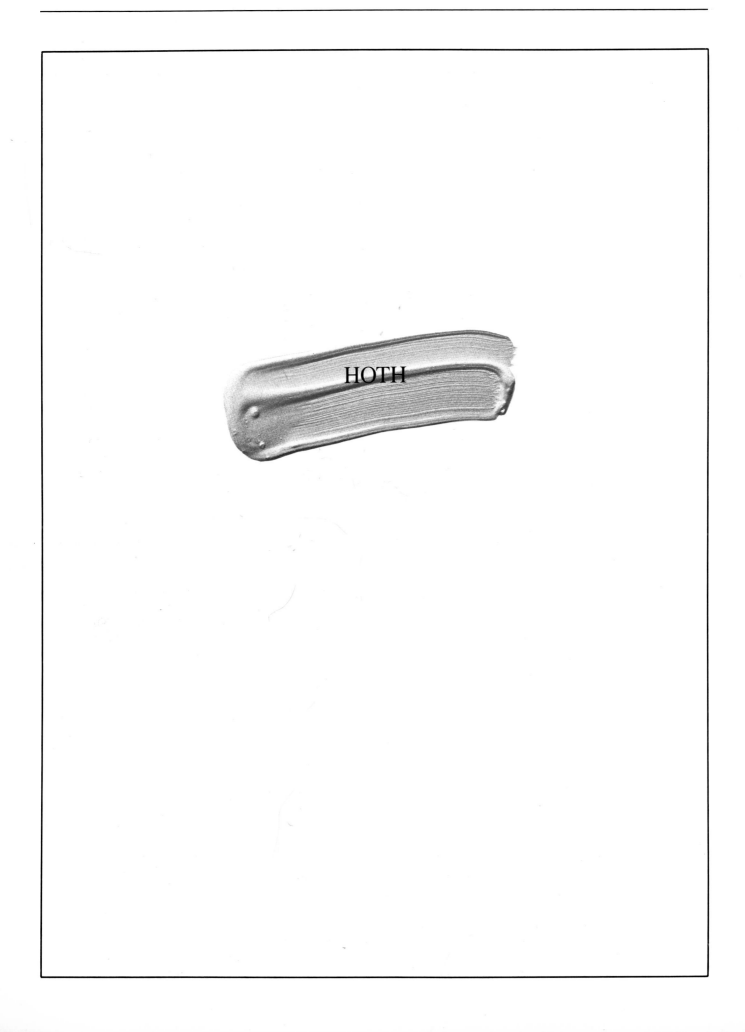

HOTH

After the destruction of the Empire's Death Star, the Rebels are relentlessly pursued by Darth Vader and his fleet of Imperial Star Destroyers. Luke Skywalker, Princess Leia, Han Solo, Chewbacca, See-Threepio, Artoo-Detoo and fellow Rebels unite on Hoth, a frozen piece of tundra spinning through space on the outer fringes of a distant galaxy.

The Rebels have blasted into the frozen landscape and created huge caverns to provide them with shelter from Hoth's harsh environment. Rebel scouting parties routinely explore the vast windswept plains and search for signs of life or any other presence on the planet.

Everything designed for the scenes on Hoth in THE EMPIRE STRIKES BACK had to depict the feeling of a frozen wilderness. The clothing had to look as if it could provide protection from the cold. Quilted fabrics and parkalike jackets with fur-lined hoods seemed appropriate. Energy packs with life-support capabilities were added to the gear the Rebels carried whenever away from their base. Breather hoods were created for the weather-proofed stormtrooper costumes. Hoth's creatures would need a thick layer of protective fat and fur. The heavy body of the Imperial All Terrain Armored Transport was designed to be supported by strong legs with a wide base to provide a distribution of weight for movement upon Hoth's icy crust. Since landspeeders on Hoth would be impractical, a wedge-shaped snowspeeder was designed to easily maneuver in the strong winds of Hoth.

Good ideas for the planning of Hoth, as elsewhere, were taken where they could be found and this meant tapping the minds of all the artists working on the film.

Many ideas were exchanged during the development of the Tauntaun and several people were involved in the process. The Tauntaun was first conceived of as a fierce, hairless reptile, then an ostrichlike mammal and later a vicious rodentlike animal. This sensitive and cognizant animal evolved into a furry, steedlike creature. Animated by Phil Tippett, the Tauntaun is also a creature of significant importance in the field of stop-motion animation.

The script called for the Tauntaun to be running in almost all of its shots, which could be very difficult using a stop-motion technique. Stop-motion animation is similar to the effect that would be created by shooting many still pictures and running them through a projector at a very fast shutter speed. Each frame contains a single, crystal sharp image and when

the film is projected a funny kind of staccato movement is produced. A running horse in a motion picture appears to be real because the motion picture film inadequately captures the movement, and the legs therefore are blurred. Simulating the blurring effect in stop-motion adds to the realism. To achieve this effect the Tauntaun model was moved during the shooting of each frame. Each time the shutter of the camera opened to shoot one frame, the Tauntaun puppet was moved physically. This technique, never done before in the field of stop-motion animation, was accomplished by using a computerized track to free the animator's hands and give him more time to concentrate on the creature's subtler gestures and movements.

The All Terrain Armored Transport (AT-AT), fondly known as the walker, is an Imperial attack vehicle fifty feet high and functions as the centerpiece for many spectacular battle sequences in the film. The actual construction of such a monstrous machine to scale was found to be impractical. The realistic look of the walkers created in miniature in the film is a credit to the ILM special effects artists and technicians.

Lucas felt the combination of the walker's mechanical design with its animallike movements would have a very ominous effect. The walker appears to move as if it were a large animal stalking prey. Initially designed by Joe Johnston, the outer appearance of the body and head took its final shape while under construction in the model shop at ILM. Engineering the AT-AT into an operational stop-motion model was the pet project of Jon Berg, who was responsible for the inner working patterns and animation of the walker. Various large animals were filmed and their leg movements analyzed in order to lend their characteristic movements to the model walkers. At the same time, prototype models were also videotaped and filmed in order to study various movement problems. But even with all the pre-planning, it was the models themselves that eventually determined their style of locomotion.

The walkers originally were to be filmed separately and then matted into the live action footage from the location shooting in Norway. As the test footage was developed, Lucas was disappointed with the shallow image created by shooting the white AT-AT models against a white snow background. This caused a temporary setback to all the work that had been done on the walker battle sequence over a period of two years. No one wanted a compromise in the sequence's visual impact. To solve the problem, Lucas turned to a talented young artist named Mike Pangrazio to paint realistic snow landscapes. These background paintings could be matched up with the live-action plate to give the sequence the added visual impact that was necessary.

To complete the effect, Nilo Rodis-Jamero built miniature snow sets to fill out the landscape. Using an elaborate system of pulleys, wenches and trap doors, he made it possible for Jon Berg to reach the models at all times

Matte painting of Hoth and its moons, Mike Pangrazio

1

while they were being filmed. It was on these miniature sets that Jon Berg worked closely with all members of his department. They had to make the eighteen inch and four and a half feet tall models look like fifty feet tall attack vehicles that move with sinister grace. The miniatures later matched the full scale section of the walker built in England around which the live action was shot.

Inspired by the challenge, these artists continued their collaborative effort until the desired effects were completed for the film.

2

1
Production painting,
Ralph McQuarrie;
Joe Johnston, in collaboration with Ralph McQuarrie, designed the ultra-sensory, investigating probe robot which drifts over the surface of Hoth. Like an arachnid, it has long leglike extensions that can reach down and pick up things from the ground as well as draw things in close to its body. The legs are constantly touching ground and pushing off and gesture in a way which makes the Probot appear to be alive. The lenses, like eyes, are also sensing devices. The Probot is armed with laser weapons and can not only defend itself but will self destruct to protect the information that it has gathered. When it is confronted by Chewie, the Probot acts like a gun-fighter and whips around to shoot.

The arctic landscape was inspired by pictures of an ice field which had broken up in the spring and had then frozen over. The yellowish sky is similar to the color sometimes seen in arctic regions.
2
Probot emerging from pod,
Norman Reynolds

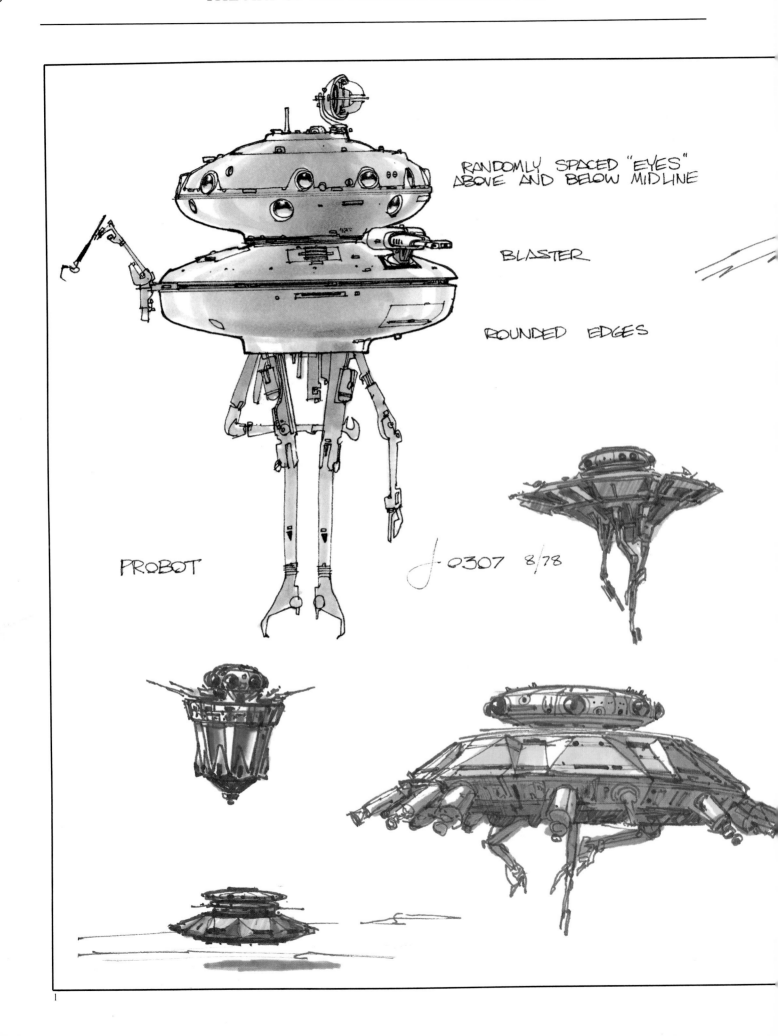

RANDOMLY SPACED "EYES"
ABOVE AND BELOW MIDLINE

BLASTER

ROUNDED EDGES

PROBOT

J-0307 8/78

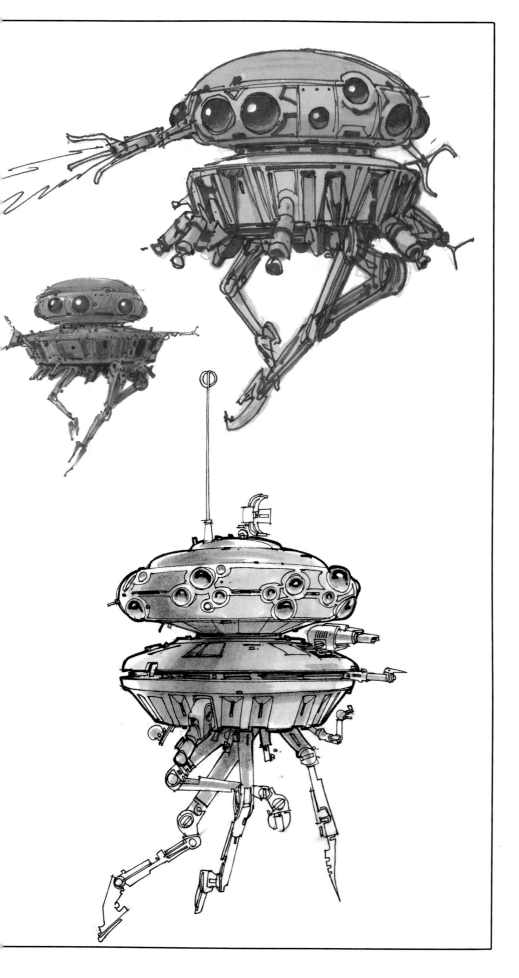

1
Probot sketches, Ralph McQuarrie and
Joe Johnston

1

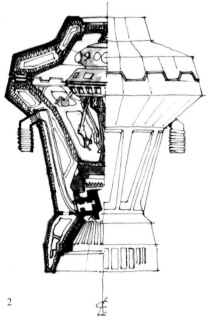

2

1
Sketch for production painting,
Ralph McQuarrie
2
Probot pod sketch, Norman Reynolds
3
Photograph of Probot, George Whitear
4
Preliminary Probot design,
Alan Tomkins under the direction
of Norman Reynolds
1 ▶
Hoth background painting,
Mike Pangrazio
2 ▶
Photograph of Mike Pangrazio by
Howard Stein
3-5 ▶
Hoth background paintings,
Mike Pangrazio

3

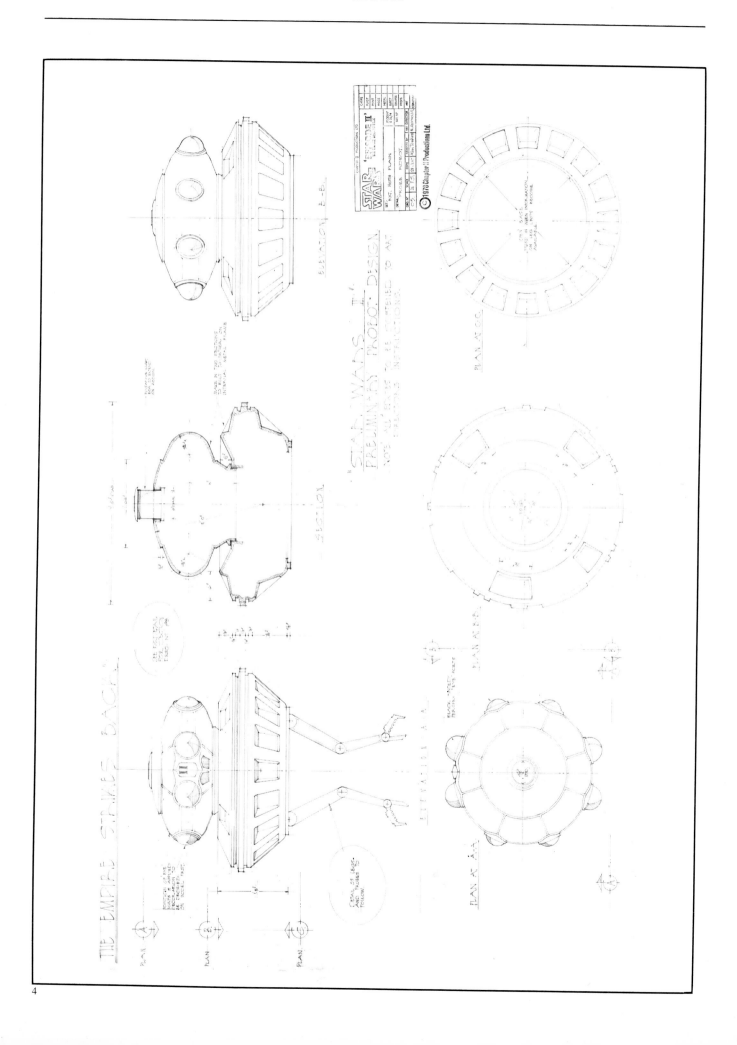

1

2

3

4

5

1

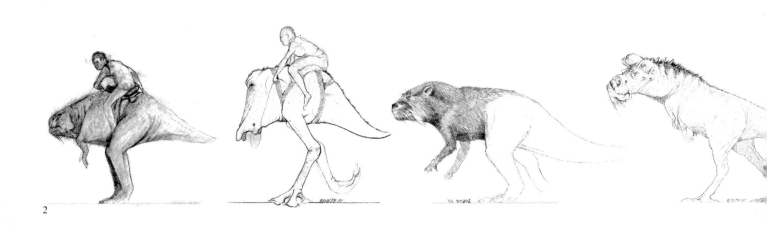

2

1
Production painting,
Ralph McQuarrie;
Luke and the Tauntaun have just ridden
to a ridge when the low, moaning growl
of a Wampa Ice Creature captures their
attention. In this conception the Taun-
taun is similar to a beast of burden. It
has the ears and nose of a camel, horns
of a yak or other mountain animal and
the rest is kangaroo or dinosaurlike. It
has long fur around the neck and soft
down around its belly. Tauntauns are
an integral part of the life of Hoth.

The general effect of this illustration
was to be somewhat reminiscent of an
old-time western hero and his trusty,
beloved horse.

2
Preliminary sketches for Tauntaun,
Phil Tippett

1

2

3

4

5

6

1-2
Preliminary drawings for Tauntaun,
Joe Johnston
3-7
Preliminary drawings,
Ralph McQuarrie

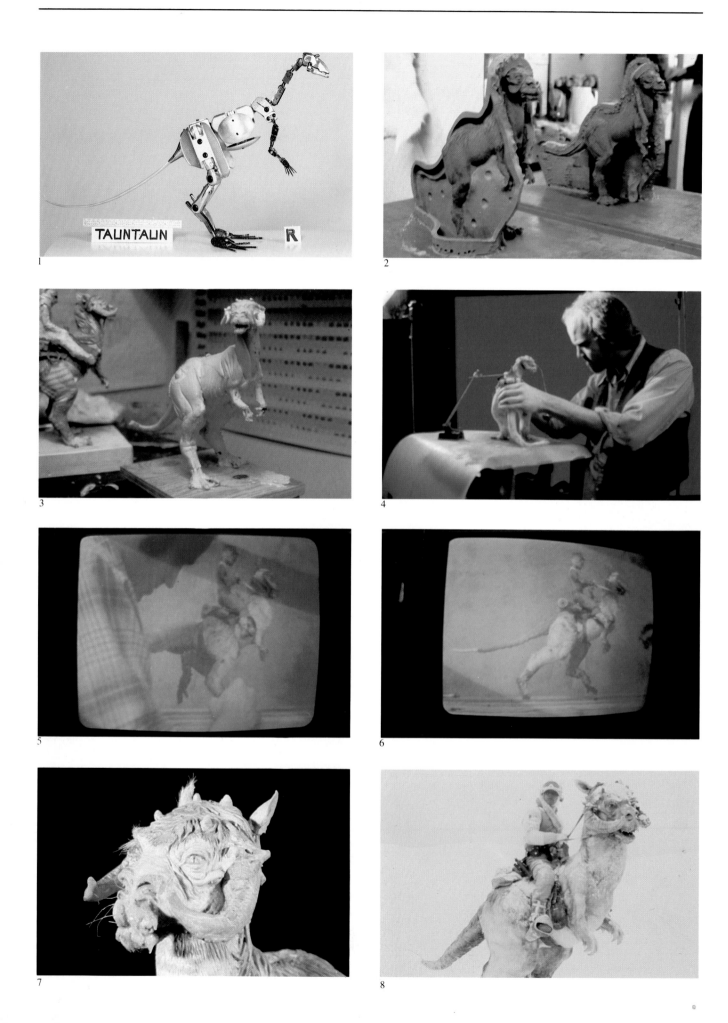

9

1

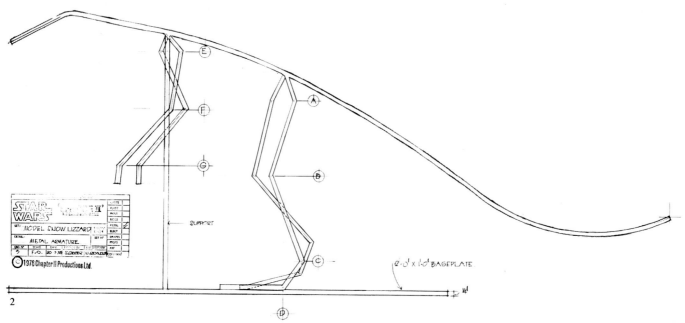

2

1
Production painting,
Ralph McQuarrie;
McQuarrie chose a canyon as the set-
ting when he was asked to illustrate the
Imperial walkers chasing Luke on his
Tauntaun. In this painting, Luke has
just ridden up a ravine on his Tauntaun
and, surprised by the walkers, he turns
to run for his life. In this painting, the
Tauntaun's sleek, muscular legs enable
it to leap like a deer when confronted
by the walker's laser blasts. During this
stage of development, the Tauntaun
was thought of as being dinosaurlike
and potentially vicious yet still willing
to obey commands.

The Imperial walkers in this painting
represent an early concept and are
based on the drawings of Joe Johnston.
2
Metal armature diagram of early
Tauntaun, Steve Cooper under the
direction of Norman Reynolds

1

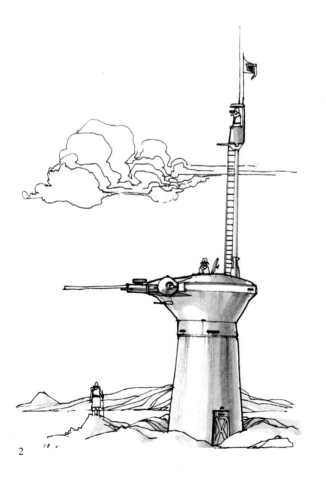

2

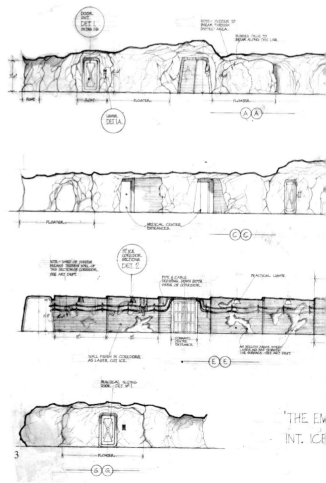

3

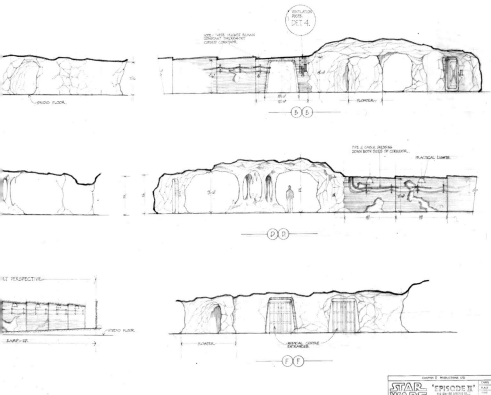

1
Production painting,
Ralph McQuarrie;
The entrance to the Rebel hangar is hidden from view by a great slab of fallen glacial ice. McQuarrie studied many ice formations and glaciers before doing the painting. For dramatic composition, he painted the frozen cliffs in the background a cold blue to create contrast with the white ice.

The revolving Rebel turret is operated by people inside. The soldier on top acts as a tank gunner and his weapon is close for fighting. A Tauntaun and rider, probably Han, are shown for scale.
2
Sketch of Rebel laser cannon turret,
Joe Johnston
3
Elevation of ice corridor,
Ted Ambrose under the direction of Norman Reynolds

1

2

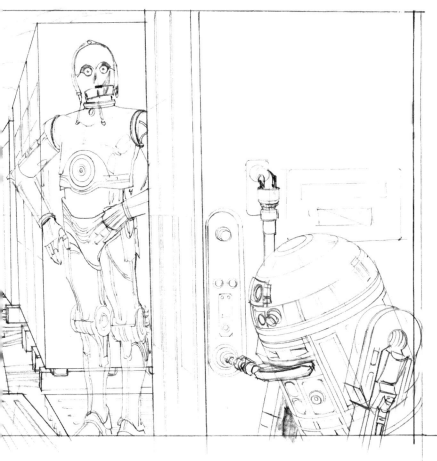

1
*Production painting,
Ralph McQuarrie;*
*The nerve center of the Rebel base is
hidden inside the honeycomb network
of the ice cave complex. Temporary
and portable field equipment has been
brought in by the soldiers manning the
radar consoles. Daylight filters through
the cracks in the ceiling of the tunnel.
The tunnels were probably formed naturally. Powerpacks line the walls
opposite the constantly alert Rebels.
The floor is covered with vacuum-
formed duckboards and is similar to the
covering used on the airfields and
muddy areas during World War II.*

*See-Threepio and Artoo-Detoo, not
present in many of the production
paintings, were included in this
painting.*
2
*Sketch for production painting,
Ralph McQuarrie*

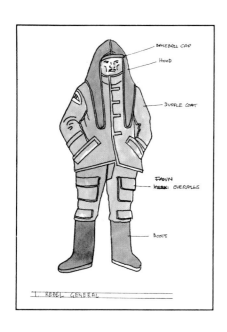

BASEBALL CAP

HOOD

DUFFLE COAT

FAWN ~~KHAKI~~ OVERALLS

BOOTS

1. REBEL GENERAL

CLOTH HELMET

KHAKI QUILTED JACKET·

~~KHAKI~~ FAWN OVERALLS

BOOTS

2. CONTROLLERS ETC

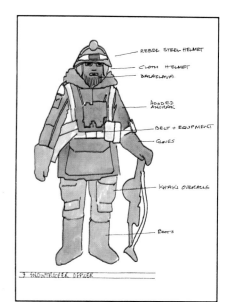

REBEL STEEL HELMET

CLOTH HELMET

BALACLAVA

HOODED ANORAK

BELT + EQUIPMENT

GLOVES

KHAKI OVERALLS

BOOTS

3. SNOWTROOPER OFFICER

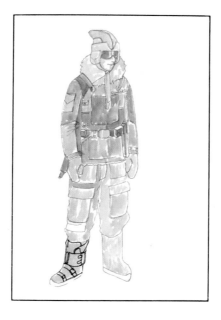

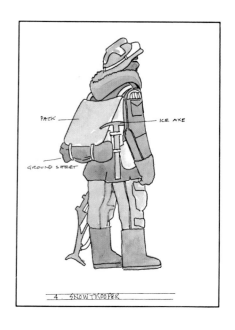

PACK

ICE AXE

GROUND SHEET

4. SNOWTROOPER

BASEBALL CAP
CLOTH HELMET
HOODED ANORAK
GLOVES
FAWN OVERALLS
BOOTS

GROUND CREWMAN

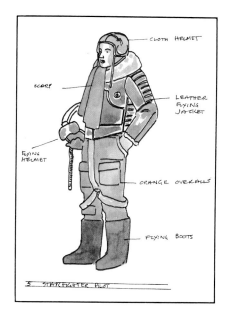

CLOTH HELMET
SCARF
LEATHER FLYING JACKET
FLYING HELMET
ORANGE OVERALLS
FLYING BOOTS

5 STARFIGHTER PILOT

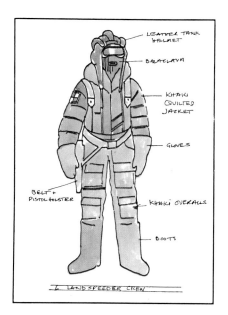

LEATHER TANK HELMET
BALACLAVA
KHAKI QUILTED JACKET
GLOVES
BELT + PISTOL HOLSTER
KHAKI OVERALLS
BOOTS

6. LANDSPEEDER CREW

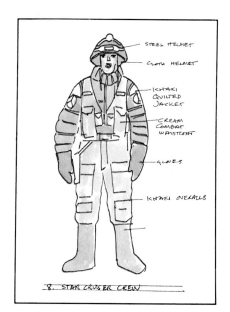

STEEL HELMET
CLOTH HELMET
KHAKI QUILTED JACKET
CREAM COMBAT WAISTCOAT
GLOVES
KHAKI OVERALLS

8. STAR CRUISER CREW

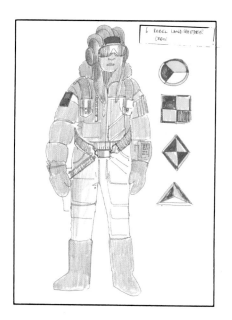

6 REBEL LANDSPEEDER CREW

Costume sketches, John Mollo

1

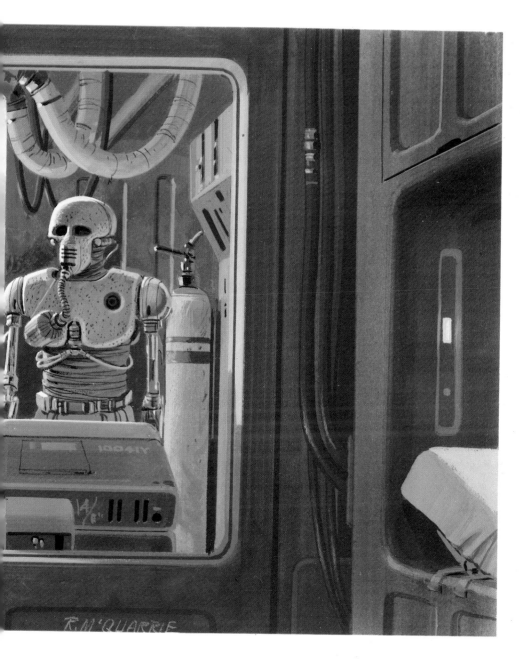

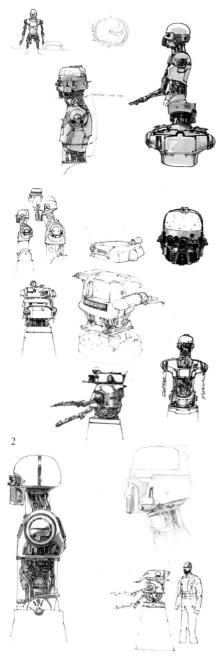

1
Production painting,
Ralph McQuarrie;
After Luke's overnight exposure to
Hoth's fierce environment he is placed
in a bacta tank. Han and Leia await
their friend's rejuvenation from an
adjoining room. The medical staff is
headed by Too-Onebee, a medical droid
with a human brain. The ultimately
logical surgeon, its mechanical support
system is backed up with a micro-
processing computer.
2
Thumbnail sketches of Too-Onebee,
Ralph McQuarrie

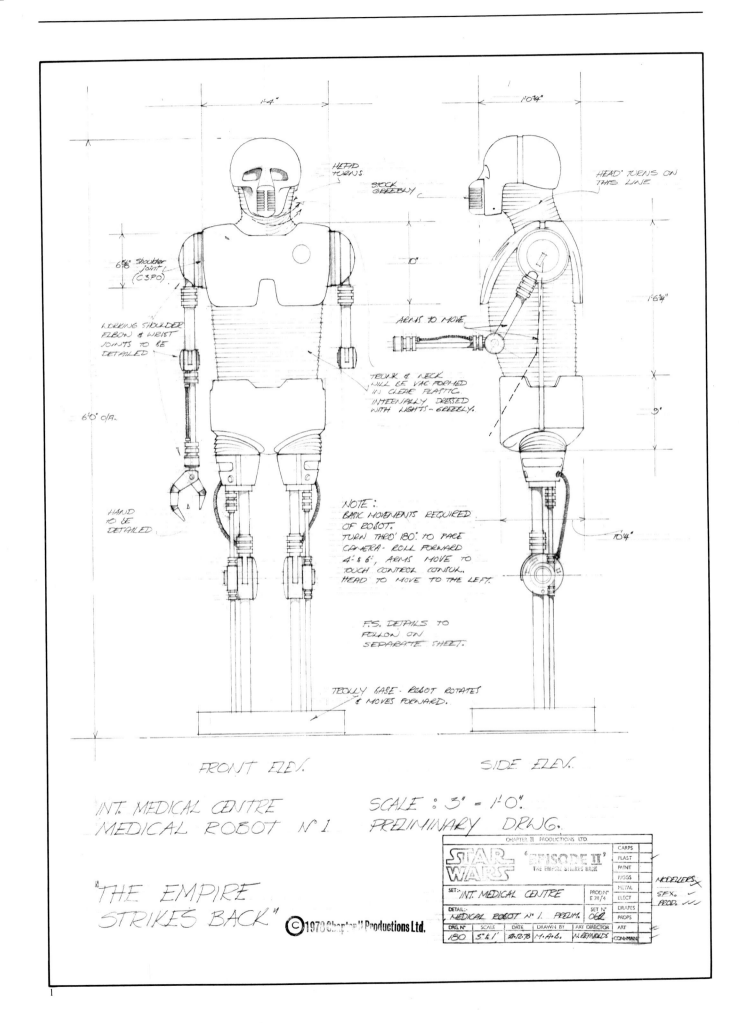

FRONT ELEV.   SIDE ELEV.

INT. MEDICAL CENTRE SCALE : 3" = 1'0".
MEDICAL ROBOT N° 1 PRELIMINARY DRWG.

"THE EMPIRE
STRIKES BACK" © 1978 Chapter II Productions Ltd.

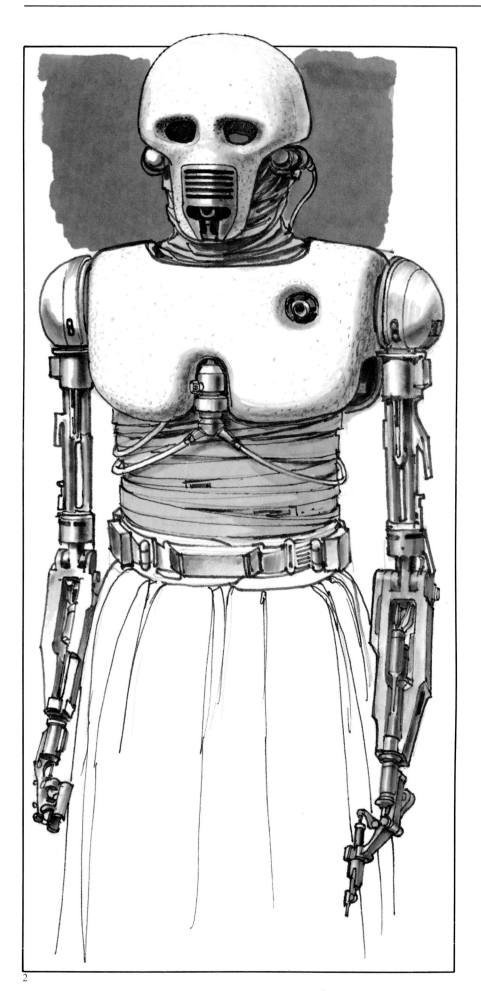

2

1
Preliminary drawing of Too-Onebee,
Michael Boone under the direction of
Norman Reynolds
2
Sketch of Too-Onebee,
Ralph McQuarrie

1

2

4

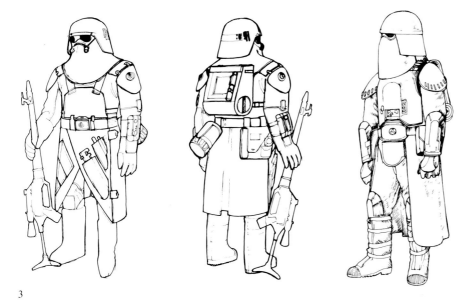

1
Production painting,
Ralph McQuarrie;

The battle for control of the Rebel generator was fought by troops on foot. At an early stage in story development, it was planned that the generator would be a matte painting and, therefore, it was placed at the top of the picture to keep it separate from the live action plate.

Joe Johnston and Ralph McQuarrie both worked on designs for the Imperial stormtroopers. The mask over the stormtrooper's face has a breathing device to warm the air. Johnston added the hood that covers the trooper's neck and also designed the laser rifles. On the stormtrooper's back is a power pack with miniaturized equipment, radios, heaters, and other survival apparatus. The unit insignia on the helmets is a graphic design of McQuarrie's.

2
Thumbnail sketches of attack on Rebel generator, Ralph McQuarrie

3
Stormtrooper costume sketches, John Mollo

4
Sketch for stormtrooper, Ralph McQuarrie

3

2

1
*Sketches and thumbnails of Rebel
generator, Ralph McQuarrie*
2
Study of stormtroopers, Joe Johnston

1

2

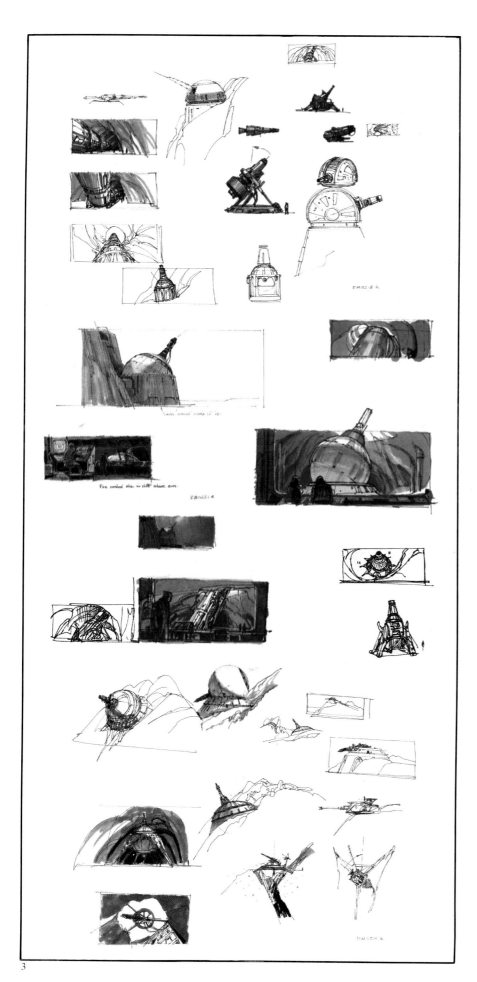

4

1, 2

Production paintings,
Ralph McQuarrie;
While working out the lighting for the
ion cannon control room, McQuarrie
decided to keep the level very low
because the Rebels would be viewing
radar screens. In the process of design-
ing the cannon, McQuarrie began
wondering about the arrangement of
the sighting and control features. It
seemed reasonable to locate them away
from the gun; anything with the power
to destroy a giant spaceship like a Star
Destroyer seemed likely to be dan-
gerous. Putting this room high in the
cliff overlooking the gun seemed logi-
cal. The windows can be seen as a
small slot above the gun in the ice cliff.
Seeing the movement of the gun
through the windows would add to the
drama of the scene.

The exterior of the ion cannon illustra-
tion was painted as a moonlit scene.
3

Thumbnail sketches for ion cannon,
Ralph McQuarrie
4
Sketch for Rebel, Ralph McQuarrie
1 ▶

Early construction drawing of ion
cannon, Michael Lamont under the
direction of Norman Reynolds
2-5 ▶
Stormtrooper costumes, Joe Johnston

3

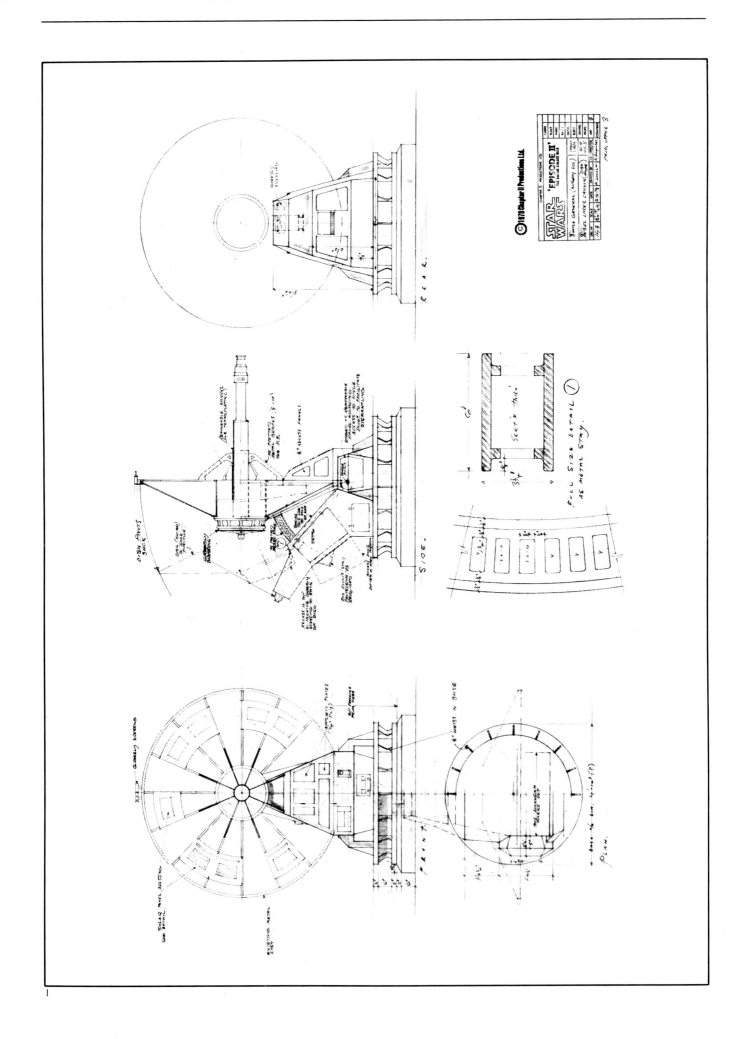

2

3

1

5

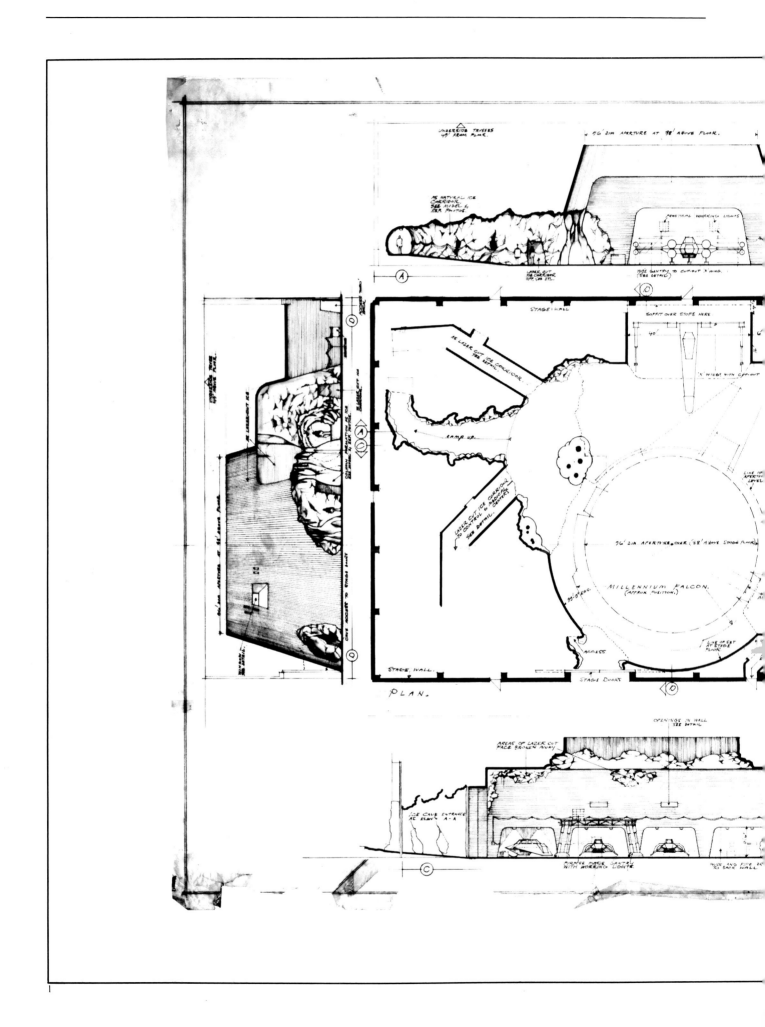

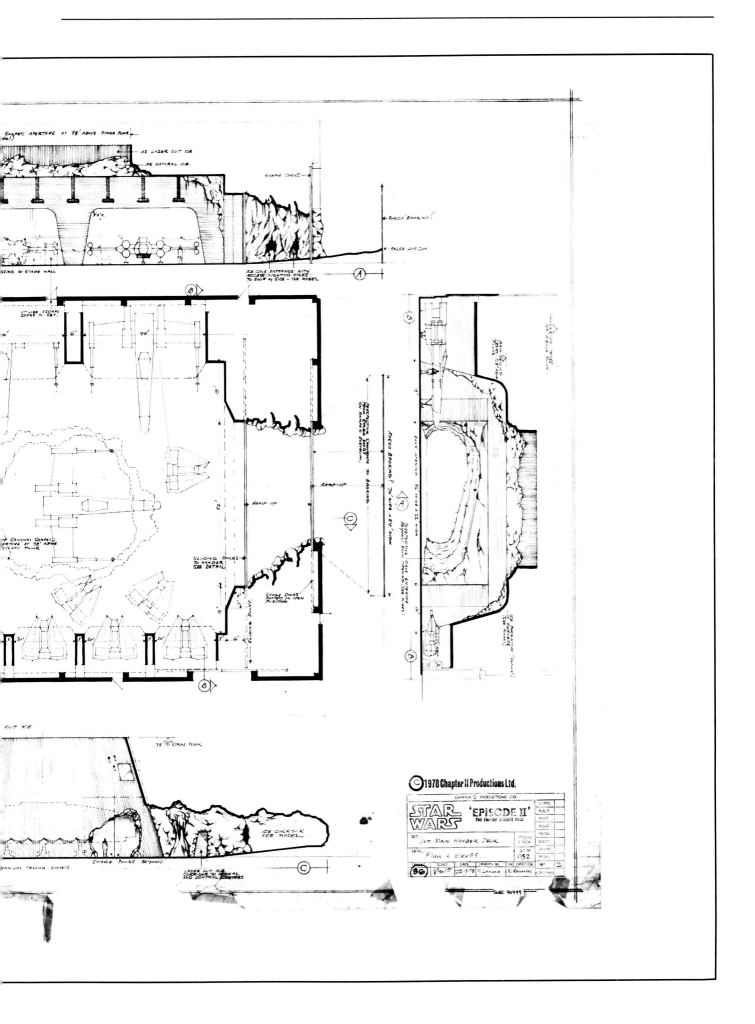

1

2

3

4

1, 7
Sketch for Rebel pilot,
Ralph McQuarrie
2, 3, 4, 6
Production paintings,
Ralph McQuarrie;
These paintings represent the interior
of the ice cave complex. They were
done to indicate where matte paintings
would be needed. Originally McQuar-
rie felt the caves would be filled with
stalagmites or other natural forma-
tions, but it was decided that the Rebels
would have laser blasted the space to
make it larger and more functional.
The serations, caused by the laser
blasting, also made it easy to blend in
matte lines. The matte paintings would
cover up the microphones, lights and
camera cranes which would be on the
live-action plate sent from England
to ILM.

The Rebels devised the complex tunnel
layout so that a direct Imperial attack
could be quickly dispersed.
5
Snowspeeder model, built under the
direction of Lorne Peterson
1 ◄
Stage plan for Rebel hangar,
Michael Lamont under the direction
of Norman Reynolds

5

6   7

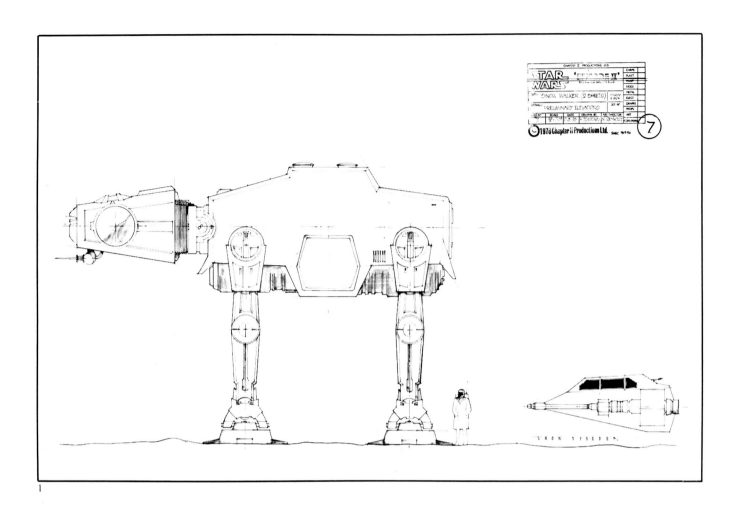

1

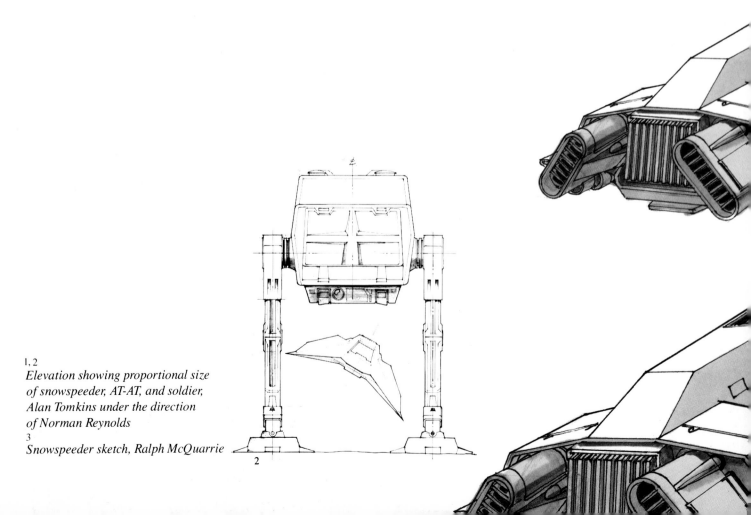

1, 2
Elevation showing proportional size
of snowspeeder, AT-AT, and soldier,
Alan Tomkins under the direction
of Norman Reynolds
3
Snowspeeder sketch, Ralph McQuarrie

2

3

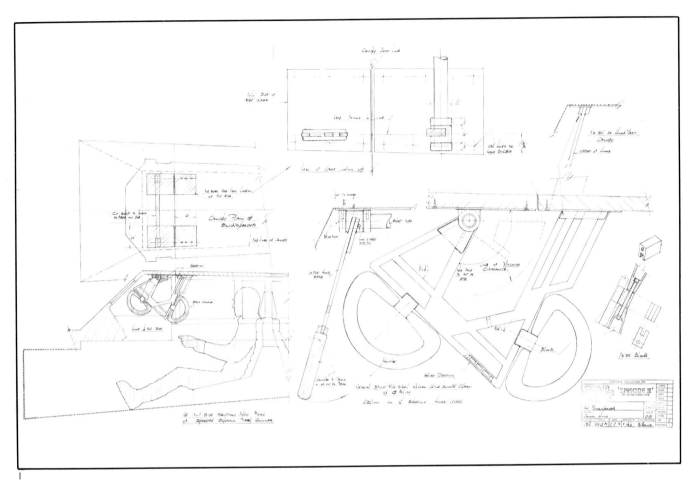

1

1, 2
*Detail construction drawing of
snowspeeder interior and canopy
hinge, Fred Hole under the direction
of Norman Reynolds*
3
*Construction drawing of snowspeeder,
Alan Tomkins under the direction of
Norman Reynolds*
1-4 ▶
*Snowspeeder models, photographs by
Terry Chostner*
5-8 ▶
*Snowspeeder elevations,
Nilo Rodis-Jamero*
9 ▶
*Drawing for camera angle
set-up from interior of snowspeeder,
Michael Lamont under the direction
of Norman Reynolds*
10 ▶
*Sketch to show placement of
pyrotechnic effects, Joe Johnston*
11 ▶
*Construction drawing for gun muzzle,
Fred Hole under the direction of
Norman Reynolds*

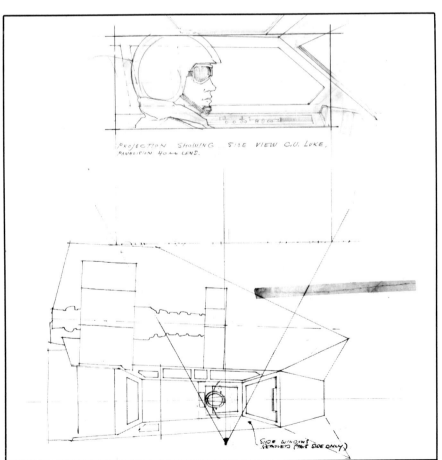

2

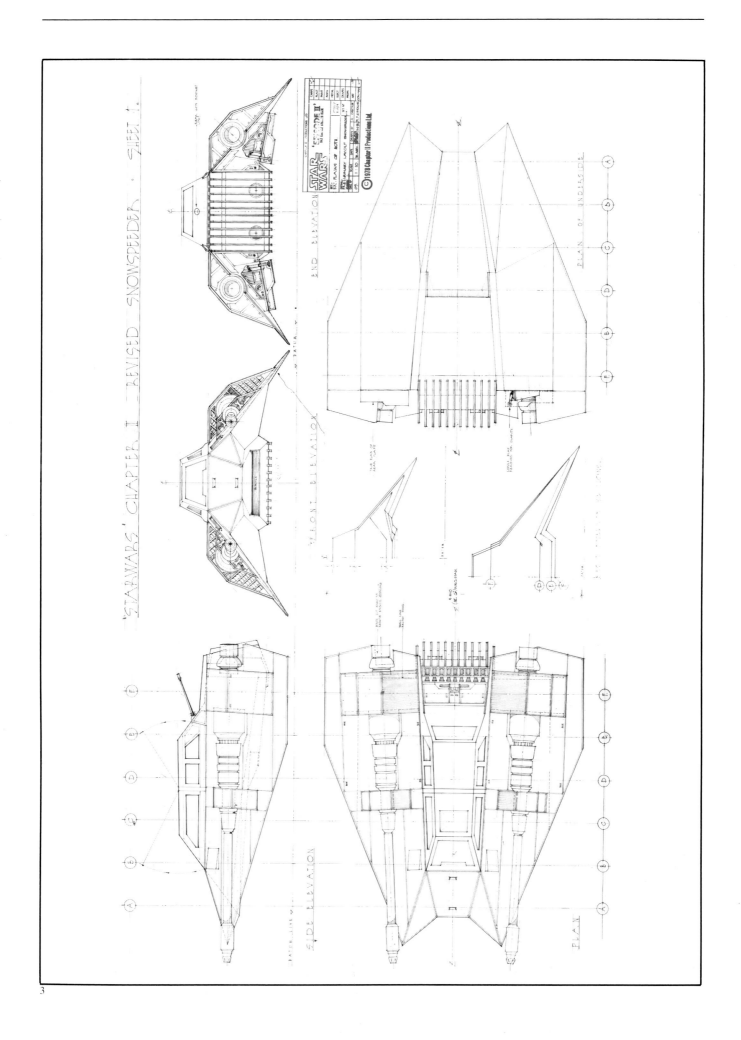

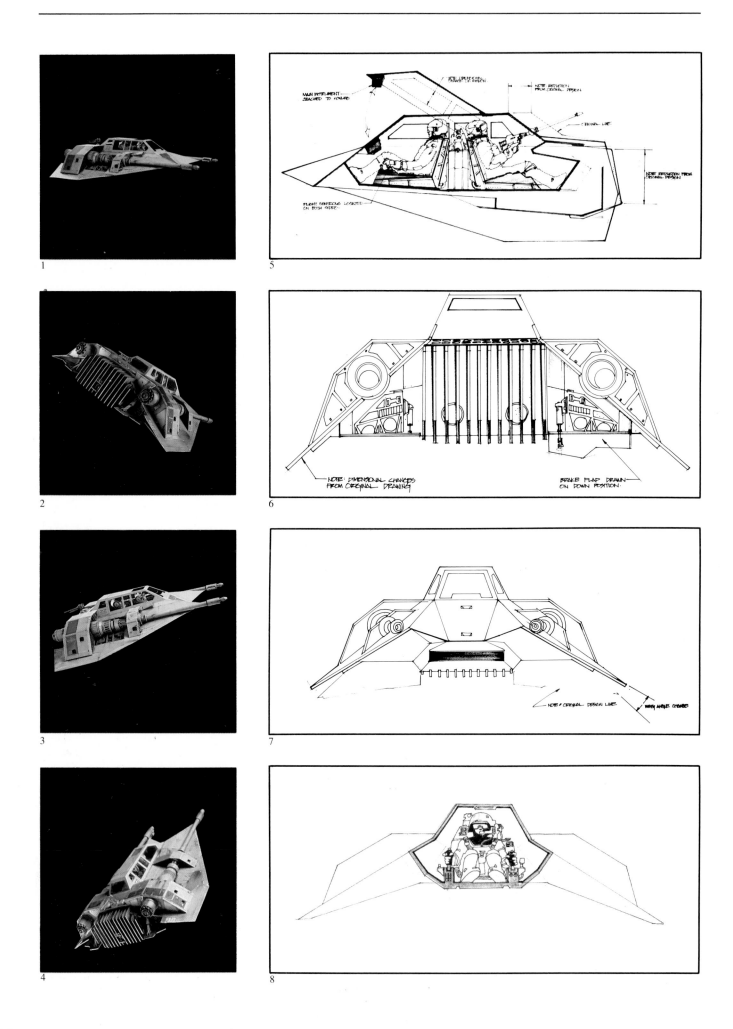

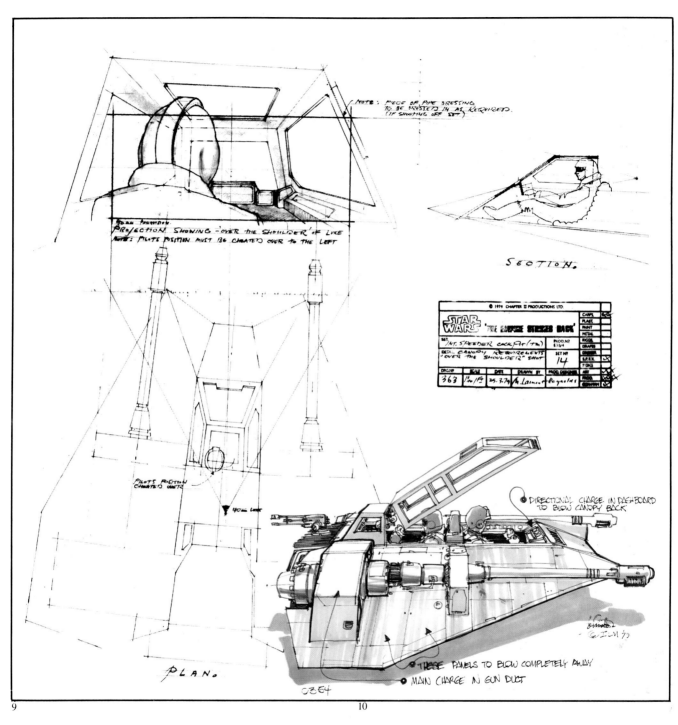

NOTE: PIECE OF PIPE DRESSING
TO BE DRESSED IN AS REQUIRED.
(IF SHOOTING OFF SET)

PROJECTION SHOWING "OVER THE SHOULDER" OF LUKE
NOTE: PILOTS POSITION MUST BE CHEATED OVER TO THE LEFT

SECTION.

PILOTS POSITION
CHEATED OVER?

40mm LENS

PLAN.

0364

DIRECTIONAL CHARGE IN DASHBOARD
TO BLOW CANOPY BACK

THESE PANELS TO BLOW COMPLETELY AWAY
MAIN CHARGE IN GUN DUCT

9

10

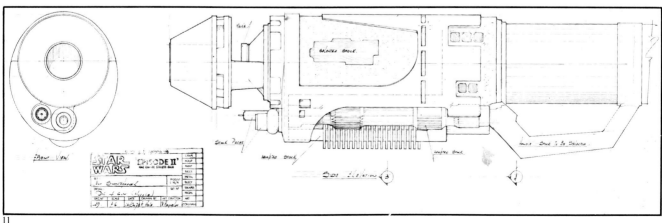

FRONT VIEW

SIDE ELEVATION

11

1

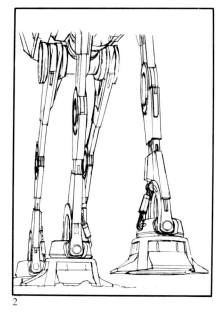

2

3

4

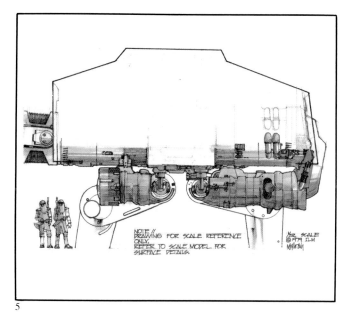

5

6

7

8

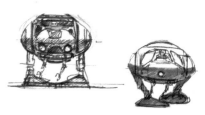

9

*I think walker should
be seen head on and
filling the space like this*

walking like this

12

10

11

1, 3
*Sketches for scout walkers,
Joe Johnston*
2, 4, 12
Sketches for AT-AT, Ralph McQuarrie
5-11
Sketches for AT-AT, Joe Johnston

1

2

3

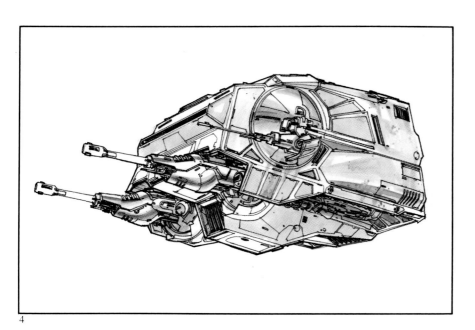

4

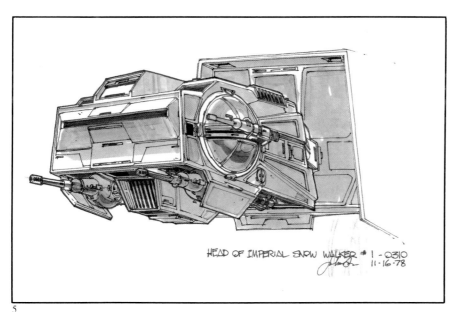

HEAD OF IMPERIAL SNOW WALKER # 1 - 0310
11·16·78

5

7

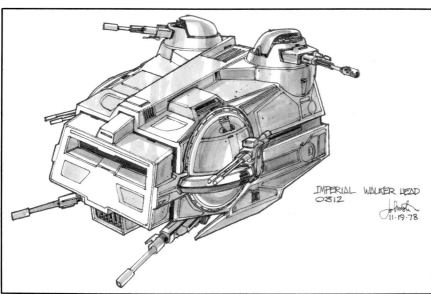

IMPERIAL WALKER HEAD
0312
11·19·78

6

1
Production paintings,
Ralph McQuarrie;
A low-flying Rebel snowspeeder passes
under the nose of a mammoth AT-AT.
The cable attached behind the speeder
is used to lash up the legs of the AT-AT,
bringing the behemoth attack vehicle to
its knees. The flames overhead come
from another speeder which has
been hit.

All the speeders are two seaters. The
radar operator doubles as a rear gun-
ner. The pilot faces forward aiming two
heavy laser cannons by pointing the
whole ship at its target, as was done
with the fighter aircraft of World
War II.
2
After making several sketches of vari-
ous aspects of the battle, McQuarrie
painted this view of the Rebel snow-
speeders circling a crippled walker.
Hit, its front legs have crumbled, knees
first, bringing it down like a large
animal. The cliffs in the background
contain the Rebel stronghold. In the
film, a battle scene like this would be
composed of live action, models and
matte paintings.
3
Downed AT-AT model, photograph by
Terry Chostner
4-6
Sketches for AT-AT head, Joe Johnston
7
Early sketch of stormtrooper,
Joe Johnston

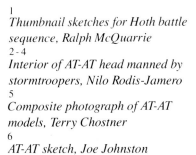

1

1
*Thumbnail sketches for Hoth battle
sequence, Ralph McQuarrie*
2 - 4
*Interior of AT-AT head manned by
stormtroopers, Nilo Rodis-Jamero*
5
*Composite photograph of AT-AT
models, Terry Chostner*
6
AT-AT sketch, Joe Johnston

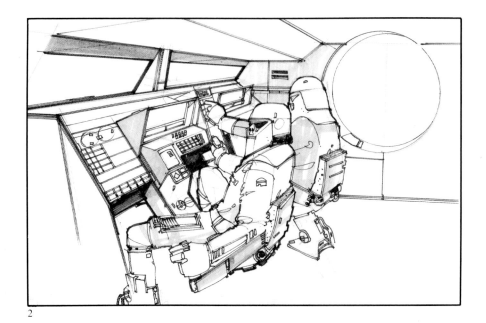

2

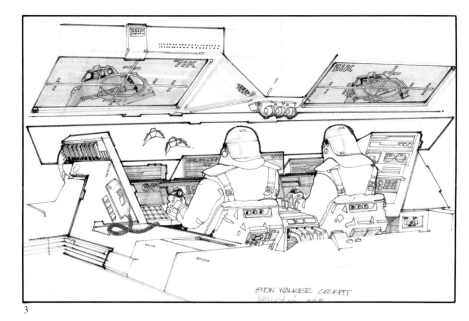

3

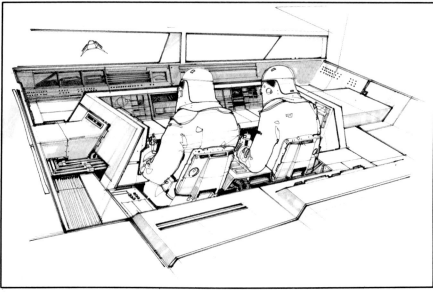

4

5

6

1
Production painting,
Ralph McQuarrie;
This is the moment when Luke scrambles out of his crashed snowspeeder and must decide if he's going to run from the charging AT-ATs before the smoke clears. Painted to complete the collection of key action shots, McQuarrie captures great detail in this moment: the bent laser cannon, the gouged furrow of ice and the smoke and steam resulting from the collision between the hot metal of the blasted speeder and the ice. This effect on film would be a combination of live action, models and matte paintings.

John Mollo designed the flight suit and gear.

1
Photograph of AT-ATs against
background painting, Don Dow;
airbrushing by Ralph McQuarrie
and Bob Jacobs

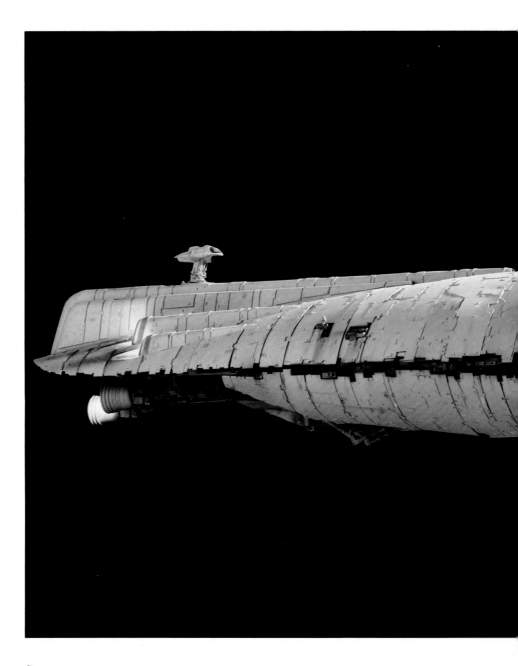

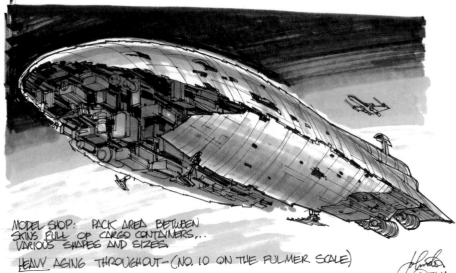

1
*Rebel Transport model, built under the
direction of Lorne Peterson*
2, 3
*Sketches of Rebel Transport,
Joe Johnston*

MODEL SHOP: PACK AREA BETWEEN
SKINS FULL OF CARGO CONTAINERS...
VARIOUS SHAPES AND SIZES.

HEAVY AGING THROUGHOUT—(NO. 10 ON THE FULMER SCALE)

0352

2

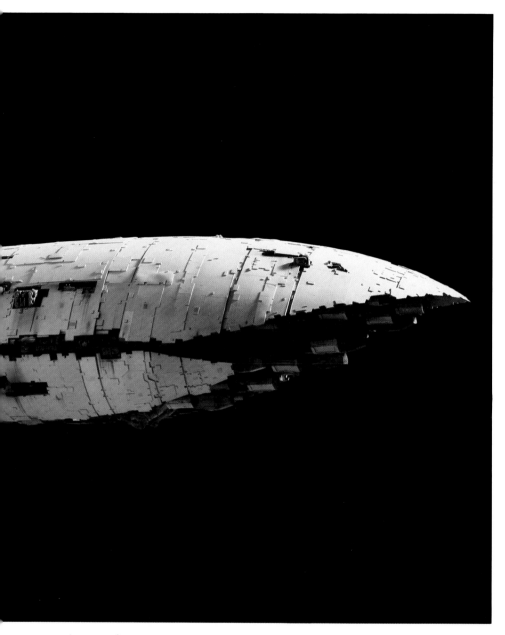

rebel transport in ice hangar / Hoth

© ILM 79

0353

3

1
Production painting,
Ralph McQuarrie;
Painted from a still photograph of the
live-action, McQuarrie tried to cap-
ture as many elements of the trench
sequences as possible. He changed the
angle and added an Imperial AT-AT
overrunning a Rebel laser turret as
snowspeeders retreat in the back-
ground.

Facing defeat, the Rebels realize that, if
not taken prisoner, it is unlikely they
will survive a frozen night on Hoth.

2
Elevation of Rebel trenches,
Michael Lamont under the direction
of Norman Reynolds

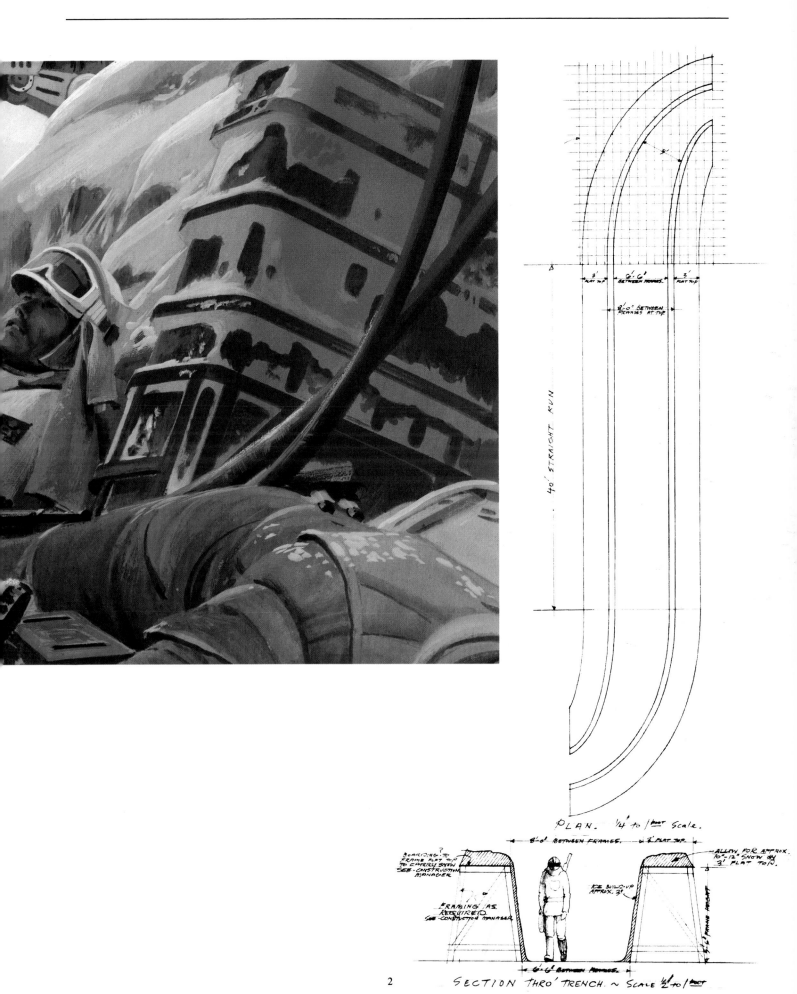

PLAN. 1/4" to 1 foot Scale.

SECTION THRO' TRENCH. ~ SCALE 1/2" to 1 foot

2

STAR DESTROYER

Led by Darth Vader in his Star Destroyer, the Executor, the Imperial fleet deploys a horde of AT-AT's to crush the Rebel encampment on Hoth.

The Executor is the Empire's top of the line vehicle with twice the destructive capability of any other craft in the Imperial fleet. Originally designed for use in a few establishing shots, Vader's Destroyer evolved into one of the film's central locations. Once the ten foot long model was placed in front of the camera and seen with its two hundred and fifty thousand lights ablaze, the storyboards were quickly changed to make the Executor one of the major vehicles in THE EMPIRE STRIKES BACK.

The scenes that take place in the Executor were filmed basically on two sets. Designed by Norman Reynolds, these sets include the control bridge and Darth Vader's private chamber. The remaining locations on the Executor were done as matte paintings. The control bridge set, with its star-filled panoramic windows, reflects Vader's unquenchable thirst for power.

Reminiscent of slave ship galleys, enlisted men work at the feet of their superiors. On this set Vader's newest and most efficient ally, Boba Fett, a bounty hunter from the Mandalore system, is introduced. Boba Fett's costume, with wrist lasers, rocket darts, and flying backpack design, is a collaboration of design efforts of Joe Johnston and Ralph McQuarrie. Built at EMI Elstree Studios in England, this suit of armor was shipped back to Johnston at ILM so that he could paint and age it.

Darth Vader's private chamber was hydraulically functional with the two halves separating like a huge pair of hands with interlocking fingers. It is in this chamber that the Lord of Sith removes his mask and contemplates his dark soul. Equipped with a direct comlink to the Emperor, Vader remains one of the most powerful beings in the galaxy.

Star Destroyer model, photograph by Nancy Moran

1

USE MOSTLY STYRENE CHIPS
FOR DETAILING... VERY FEW
KIT PARTS... NO GUNS...
ENGINE ARRANGEMENT TO BE
DETERMINED.

ILM 6·12·79

2

Production painting,
Ralph McQuarrie;
This painting was done as an establish-
ing shot for a promotional trailer
released in European theaters. We see
Hoth as a sphere of ice textured in
shades of blue and white. Painted with
camera movement in mind, there is
great perspective if you focus past the
bottom of the Star Destroyer and onto
Hoth's distant moon.
2
Sketch for Star Destroyer model,
Joe Johnston

1

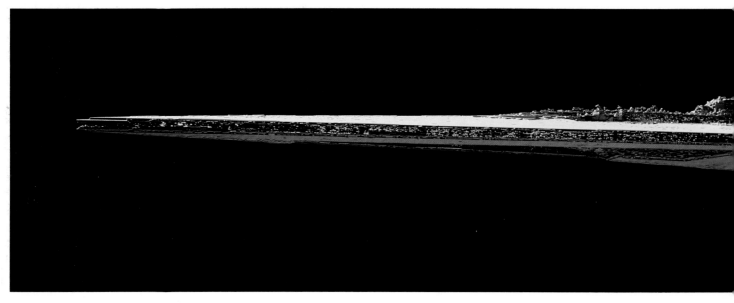

3

1, 2
Sketches of Star Destroyer bridge,
Ralph McQuarrie
3
Photograph of early Star Destroyer
model, Howard Stein
4
Darth Vader sketch, Ralph McQuarrie
1 ▶
Composite photograph of Millennium
Falcon evading the Empire's Star
Destroyer fleet. Models photographed
by Terry Chostner, airbrushing by
Ralph McQuarrie and Ron Larson.

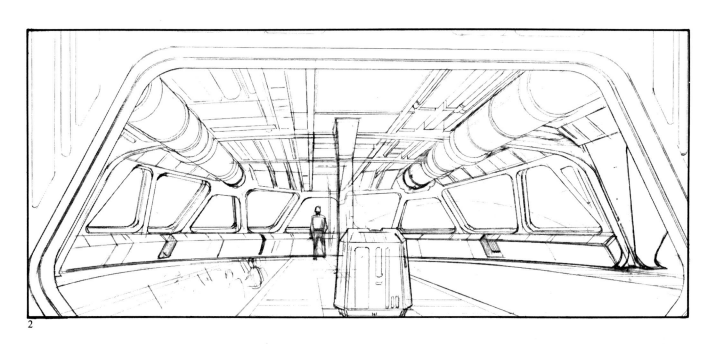

2

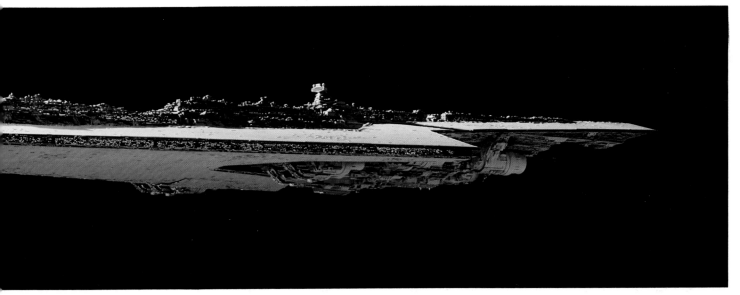

4

1

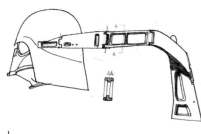

1

2

3

1, 4
Sketches of Darth Vader's meditation chamber, Norman Reynolds

2
*Production paintings,
Ralph McQuarrie;
Controls for space ships are usually shown within the heart of a vehicle for protection, but the shielding force field of the Star Destroyer allows the ship's control bridge to be at the head of the vehicle. The walkway down which Darth Vader strolls is placed low so that his view is not obstructed. McQuarrie used large windows to make the setting more dramatic and also to allow for panoramic views of planets and other passing ships.*

3
A view straight down the nose of Darth Vader's Star Destroyer is similar to the view of a cockpit of a large aircraft. In the center is a console which contains telephones and other equipment. The men at the controls operate equipment connected to various parts of the ship, such as the radar room which is located in the vehicle's interior. Overhead ducts, electronic gear and equipment panels were detailed in matte paintings for the film.

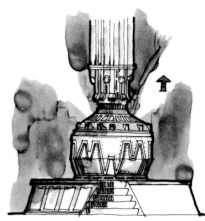

1

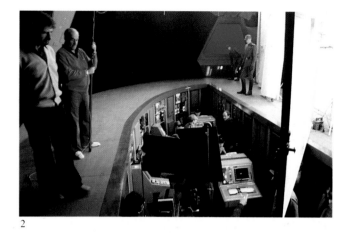

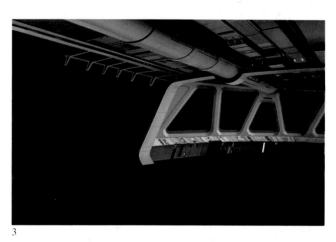

1
*Matte painting of Star Destroyer
bridge with live-action plate,
Ralph McQuarrie*

2
*Stage set of live-action plate,
photograph by George Whitear*

3
Matte painting, Ralph McQuarrie

1

2

3

4

5

8

6

7

1- 8
Studies and thumbnail sketches of meditation chamber and Emperor, Ralph McQuarrie

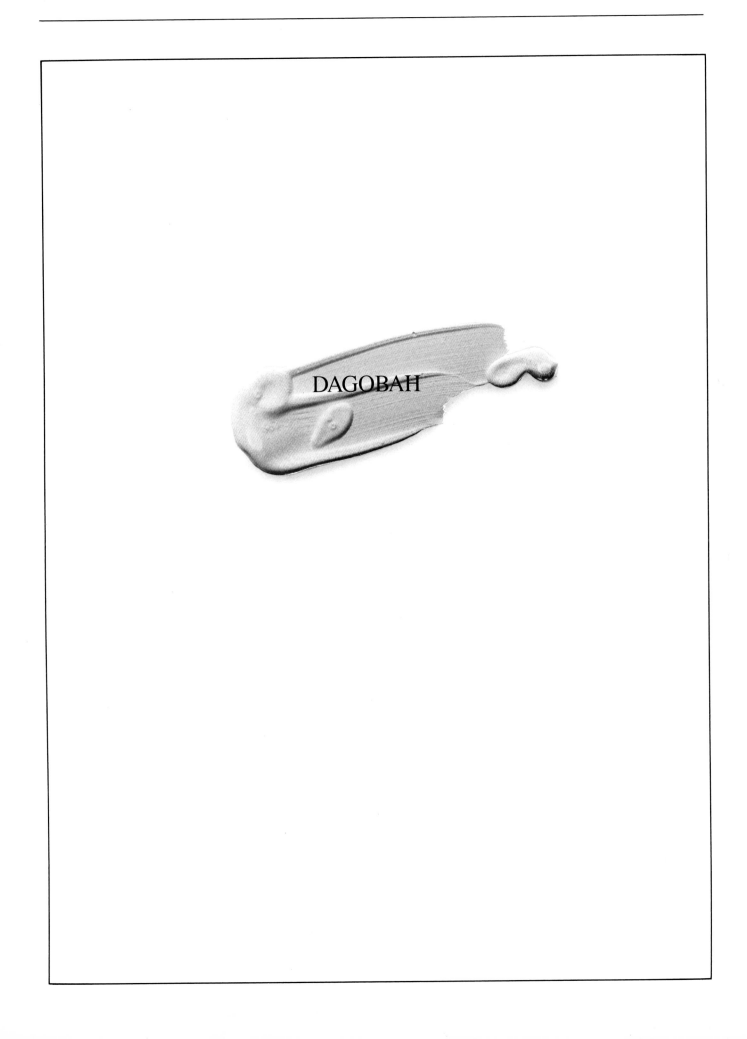

DAGOBAH

Having barely escaped the Imperial AT-AT onslaught back at Rebel base Hoth, Luke finds himself out in deep space with no planned destination. In his mind's eye he sees a strange distant planet and he can hear the echo of Obi-Wan Kenobi telling him to trust his feelings. So, with faith, Luke once more lets the Force guide his ship. His course takes him to Dagobah, a planet that is uncharted on any galactic map. Apprehensive, Luke and his co-pilot, Artoo-Detoo, slowly descend into the atmospheric mist that enshrouds the planet. As they lower their X-wing to the planet's surface they clip the tops of giant swampland trees and crash-land into a miry bog. Frantically they try to salvage their sinking craft, for it is their only means of escape from this fog-ladened world of quagmires and lagoons. During their struggle they are unknowingly observed by Yoda, an eight hundred year old Jedi sage. Out of friendship for Obi-Wan Kenobi Yoda will make sure that no harm befalls the young warrior, and more importantly, it is he who will decide whether Luke is worthy of further spiritual teaching in the ways of the Force.

There was a short moment in time when entrance to this mystical land of make-believe could actually be obtained here on the planet Earth. By a quirk of metaphysical law, between the months of August and October in the year nineteen hundred and seventy-nine, by entering the sound stages at EMI Elstree Studios in England, one could transcend space and imagination to arrive worlds away at Yoda's mystic dwelling place, the bog planet Dagobah.

Lucas wanted Dagobah to be a dark and spooky jungle swamp planet with many hidden secrets. At one point shooting on location in real swamplands was considered. Associate producer Robert Watts searched the swamps of Florida, South America, the Caribbean, and East Africa for locations. The filmmakers finally decided that if an actual swamp was to be used the production factors would be too risky and that the final look would be too earthbound. So, they devised a swamp of their own and inhabited it

with the vermin of their imaginations. Conceptual artist Ralph McQuarrie painted the earliest vision of this ever so eerie environment and picked up on the idea of giant banyan trees, which are common in swamps throughout the world. These massive trees have exposed root systems which grasp onto the eroded soil. It was thought that the exposed roots of the trees on Dagobah would be petrified in grotesque forked and gnarled shapes after millenniums of standing bare to the

elements. Once an overall design direction for Dagobah was agreed upon, it became production designer Norman Reynolds' responsibility to create this primitive world so that it could be filmed.

Like the working situation in California, those involved in the design in England worked on many worlds at once. Hoth might be on one stage while Bespin was being built on another. A typical day for Reynolds would begin with checking the progress of the work done on all of the soundstages and making whatever alterations were needed. Some of the construction was beginning on one set, some half-way through and some finishing. At one point, he was scrambling to finish six or seven sets at once.

Reynolds' first major task was to create the trees for the Dagobah forest. Although he found inspiration in McQuarrie's paintings, he decided to base his trees on those which are found in the swamps of Nigeria. He began the trees with tubular steel skeletons,

then shaped them by using wire mesh and textured them with plaster. This is similar to the process a student would use in constructing a volcano for a science fair, only this project was on a slightly larger scale. The trees stood forty feet high and were up to ten feet in circumference. Each tree was approached as a separate set unto itself. As the designer, Reynolds gave careful thought as to how the individual trees would have been affected by the elements over a long period of time.

The lagoon was to be a three foot deep, wooden pool. Because the stage floor was concrete, the pool could not be dug into the ground. This meant that the entire playing area of Dagobah had to be raised on platforms at least three feet high. The raised platforms facilitated the building of the rolling terrain, the lagoon and also made it easier to hide Yoda's operators. The use of platforms allowed Reynolds a certain amount of flexibility; the sections of the stage could be moved, thus increasing the number of variations in backgrounds and locales.

For the scene when Luke is seen climbing out of the X-wing cockpit and onto the crashed vehicle's wing, a full scale replica of the ship was constructed. When the ship was finished, it weighed thirty tons and had a magnificent forty foot wing span. The X-wing was then placed in the lagoon where it appeared partially submerged in the quagmire.

Reynolds' crew of two hundred skilled technicians and laborers worked day and night to keep construction up with the shooting schedule. Elstree Studio had been used to house all of the sets and Dagobah was the last to go up. Even as the dreaded deadline approached, things could not be rushed to the point of compromising the effect. Prop people were sent out to scour the countryside in a twenty mile radius around the studio for turf and vines to dress the set. They sent back truckload after truckload of vines locally known as "old man's beard." These can be seen draped throughout the jungle. Thousands of pieces of turf

Matte painting of Dagobah,
Mike Pangrazio

1

1

were turned upside down to create the marshy ground. Once the set was dressed with all the vegetation it came to life. Even the film equipment scattered around its perimeters, cameras on cranes, overhanging cables for microphones and the huge arc lights all looked quite grand. When it was finished the total set filled an area approximately the size of two and a half football fields. Though not a Guinness Book recordbreaker, it was one of the world's largest soundstage sets.

This eerie environment became Yoda's home. Lucas wanted Yoda to be nonhuman yet have the characteristics of an intelligent, wise old sage. He was to be the epitome of an important

mind with a calm soul. Joe Johnston drew sketches of Yoda as a wrinkled, gnomish-looking dwarf with withered hands and odd feet for tromping in the mud. Ralph McQuarrie made him less cute-looking with high pronounced cheek bones and a prominent bridge on his nose. These conceptualizations were taken to make-up artist Stuart Freeborn who sculpted the working model and gave Yoda his final character. Basically, within the skull is a very complicated mechanism that can move the eyes from side to side, up and down and around. The eyelids can be opened and closed. The ears can be twisted and moved up and down. Articulation in the mouth and teeth and

tongue can be coordinated. Yoda also has the ability to furrow his brow and make numerous other facial expressions. Frank Oz is primarily responsible for bringing Yoda to life with the assistance of Kathryn Mullen and Wendy Midener. Among them they carefully orchestrate all of Yoda's movements with their hands and fingers.

A hermit like his Jedi brother, Obi-Wan Kenobi, Yoda is an environmentalist. He is at one with the nature of the universe. It was thought that his house would have a rounded dome and be mosque- or church-like. His house is a temple of environmental efficiency, made of mud, sticks, stones

R. M^cQUARRIE

impossible to operate Yoda mechanically a complete radio controlled version was used.

One of the film's more serene segments, it is from Yoda that Luke learns to control his youthful anger and begins to understand the passive strength of the Force.

2

and other naturally existing material found on Dagobah. His windows are transparent gems. Norman Reynolds found it best to use treated styrofoam, paint and stained glass to achieve this required effect.

It was important that the interior of the house represent Yoda's character. So, Reynolds placed it by a lagoon because he felt Yoda would appreciate the falling rain. Yoda would not use technical appliances. Everything, including his furniture and storage spaces, had to seem handcrafted by Yoda. Even the scrolls that hang on the walls looked as though they were in his own hand.

Miniature clay models of the set and characters were used to figure out lighting and camera angles in Yoda's small hut. Also, it was important to know what movements puppet master Frank Oz and actor Mark Hamill would have to re-create for the story-line. Such a limited space, with so many various components, does not lend itself well to improvisation.

Frank Oz manipulated Yoda by sticking him on his arm and walking about. A channel had to be cut and the floor had to be removable in various places. Oz and his assistants would operate from a hole in the floor in situations where Yoda did not actually walk about. In those situations where it was

1
Production painting,
Ralph McQuarrie;
Luke frantically tries to salvage his sinking X-wing in this early concept of Dagobah's environment. Dagobah is a bog planet; the whole effect was to be dark and eerie. McQuarrie painted tangled undergrowth and giant banyan trees in this first interpretation of the swamp. At a later stage the banyan trees were considered too earthlike but the idea of trees with exposed root systems was retained. The use of fog seemed an obvious way to lend atmosphere and realism to the swamp set.
2
Sketch of Luke, John Mollo
1 ◄
Matte painting of Dagobah's surface and cloud cover, Mike Pangrazio

1

2

3

4

BOG PLANET — STARWARS STAGE   PLAN SCALE

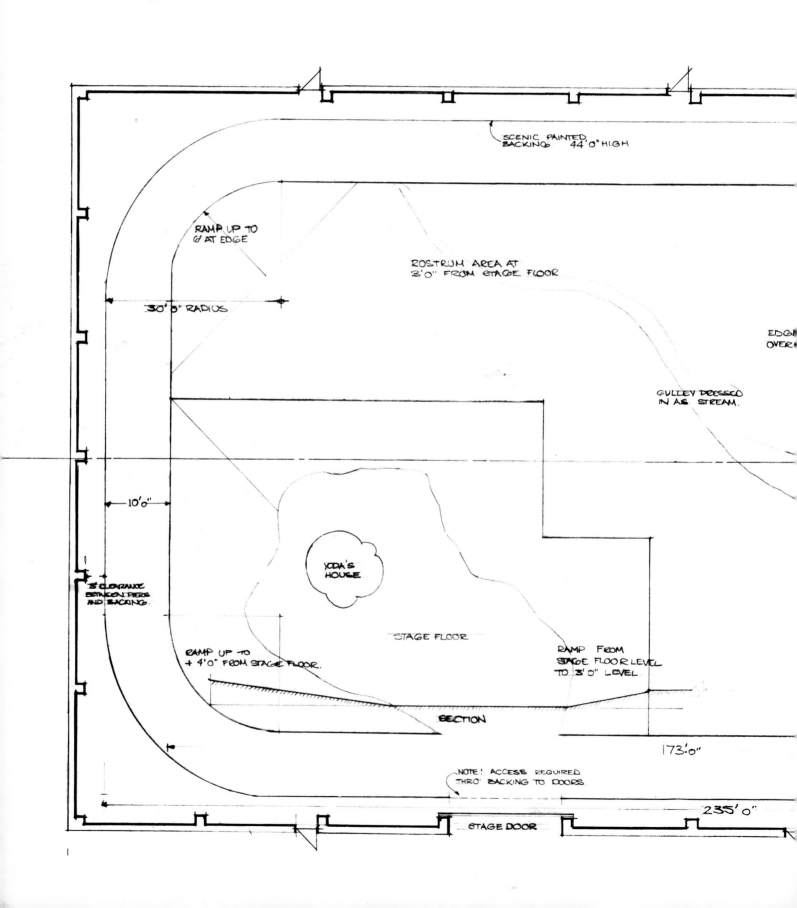

SCENIC PAINTED BACKING 44'0" HIGH

RAMP UP TO 0' AT EDGE

ROSTRUM AREA AT 3'0" FROM STAGE FLOOR

30'0" RADIUS

EDGE OVER

GULLEY DRESSED IN AS STREAM.

10'0"

YODA'S HOUSE

3' CLEARANCE BETWEEN PIERS AND BACKING.

STAGE FLOOR

RAMP UP TO + 4'0" FROM STAGE FLOOR.

RAMP FROM STAGE FLOOR LEVEL TO 3'0" LEVEL

SECTION

173'0"

NOTE! ACCESS REQUIRED THRO' BACKING TO DOORS.

235'0"

STAGE DOOR

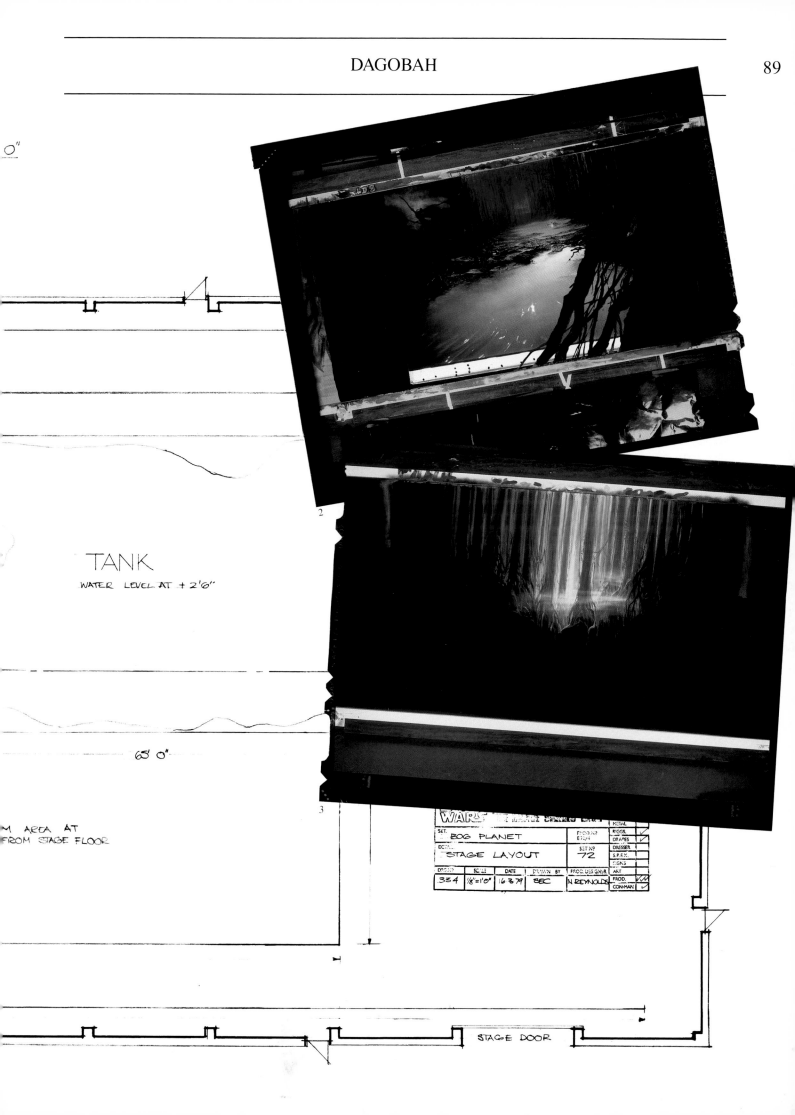

O"

TANK

WATER LEVEL AT + 2'6"

2

65 0"

3

M AREA AT
FROM STAGE FLOOR

WARS					METAL	
SET. BOG PLANET			PROD.Nº E7/4	RIGGS.	✓
DETAIL STAGE LAYOUT			SET Nº 72	DRAPES	✓
				DRESSER	
				S.P.F.X.	
				SIGNS	
DRGNº 334	SCALE 1/8"=1'0"	DATE 16 3 79	DRAWN BY SEC	PROD. DESIGNER N REYNOLDS	ART	
				FROD.	✓✓
				CON-MAN	✓

STAGE DOOR

1
Sketch of Yoda, Joe Johnston
2, 4
Head studies for Yoda,
Ralph McQuarrie
3
Head studies, Joe Johnston

1

2

3

4

1

2

3

4

5

6

7

10

8

9

1-8, 10
*Developmental sketches of Yoda,
Joe Johnston*
9
Yoda sketch, Ralph McQuarrie

1

1
Production painting,
Ralph McQuarrie;
Yoda made his house out of mud and
clay. Since light from Dagobah's sun
rarely breaks through the cloud cover-
ing and thick forest, there is a hearth in
each room for warmth. Skylights and
windows filled with precious stones let
in what little light there is.

1

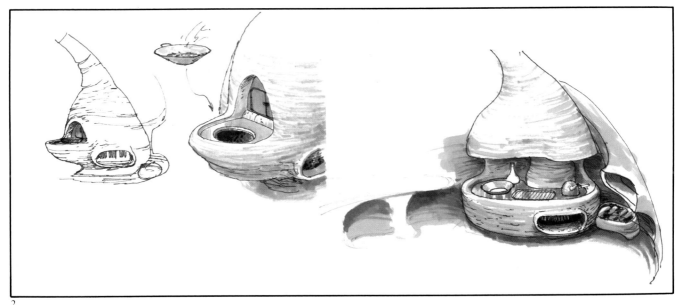

2

1
Sketch of Yoda's house in swamp forest,
Ralph McQuarrie
2, 3
Sketches for house interior,
Ralph McQuarrie

3

4

5

6

4
Production painting,
Ralph McQuarrie;
Living in a constant state of twilight,
Yoda spends most of his time in medita-
tion studying ancient documents and
diagrams. The cabinet on the wall rep-
resents one of the most technically
advanced objects in the house and
holds some of Yoda's private posses-
sions. The bottle suspended from the
ceiling holds either water or wine.
5
Sketch for production painting,
Ralph McQuarrie
6
Sketches of planet vegetation,
Ralph McQuarrie

1

2

1
Yoda's house and surrounding swamp,
photograph by Murray Close
2
Artoo-Detoo peeking into Yoda's house,
by Murray Close
3
Photograph of Yoda
by George Whitear

3

1

2

3

1
Production painting,
Ralph McQuarrie;
The air is muggy and dank as a shirt-less Luke carries Yoda on his back. The tree roots resemble claws or spider legs. Covering the ground is a field of paludial fungi with embryonic membranes. A sticky, white fluid is secreted by these "yogurt" plants. With Yoda as his guide, Luke travels through this environment on his transcendental journey of growth.
2
Thumbnail sketches for mystic tree interior, Ralph McQuarrie
3
Sketch of Luke entering mystic tree, Ralph McQuarrie

1

2

3

4

5

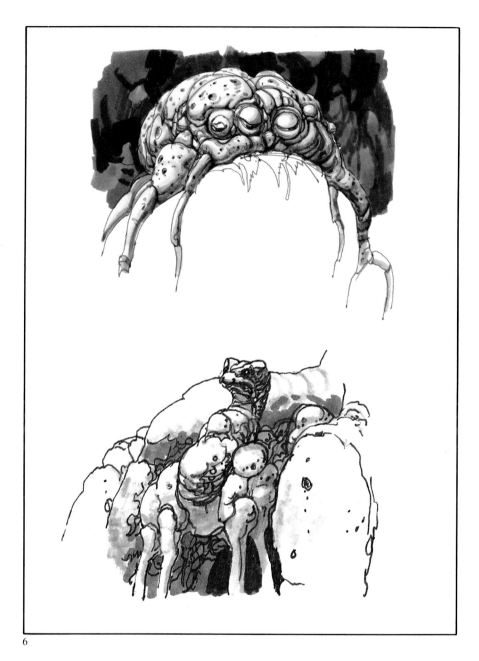

6

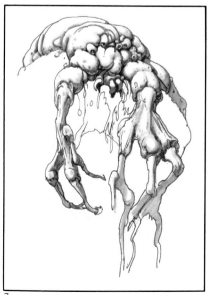

7

8

1-8
*Swamp creature sketches,
Ralph McQuarrie*

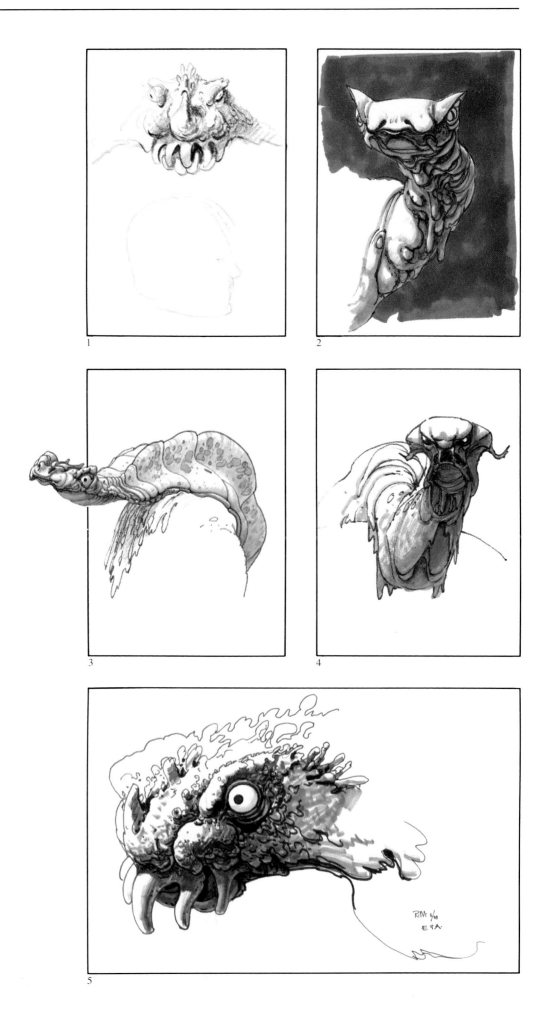

1-6
Swamp creature sketches,
Ralph McQuarrie

1

|
Production painting,
Ralph McQuarrie;
Though the scene is pictured differently in the film, McQuarrie's painting more than captures the feeling of Luke's departure from Dagobah. The young Rebel solemnly vows to his teachers that he will continue his reflections into the ways of the Jedi Knights.

Unable to get the Millennium Falcon in to hyperdrive, Han Solo decides to try his luck at outmaneuvering the attacking Imperial TIE fighters by passing through a turbulent asteroid belt.

The fast paced asteroid sequence is the cumulative work of many special effects artists combined with the work of the ILM optical department headed by Bruce Nicholson. Though the whole sequence lasts under two minutes, its construction was very complex and consisted of as many as twenty-five separate photographic elements. The asteroid sequence required extensive visual overlapping of these elements and would not have been possible without the use of an optical printer. An optical printer is a duplicating machine which is made up of several projectors and a camera. All are mounted so that the projected images can be rephotographed by the camera. This allows flexibility in changing the direction and speed of an image or in repositioning an image in a frame.

Gliding along the ridges and caverns of a large asteroid, Han ducks the Millennium Falcon into a cave and plans to wait until the Imperial forces have left the area.

The Millennium Falcon model used in the first film was four feet in diameter and weighed over one hundred pounds. This model was too heavy to use in order to make the intricate maneuvers in the asteroid sequences seem believable. A lighter, thirty pound model was constructed that could flip, twist and turn on a computerized support. A full scale Millennium Falcon, eighty feet in diameter and weighing twenty-three tons, was constructed in a shipyard in Wales for the live-action photography in England. It was built in sixteen sections for easy transport and storage and will also be used in several other STAR WARS films.

The Rebels' stay is cut short when they discover that what they have flown into is not really a cave but the mouth of a giant space slug. Though we only see the slug for a few frames, Nilo Rodis-Jamero paid special

attention to designing the right texture and scale for the model.

The animation department was headed by Peter Kuran. One responsibility of the department involved the effects of sparks and flashing lights that occur as the TIE fighters and asteroids collide during the chase of the Falcon through the asteroid belt. The animated sparks and lights were airbrushed and backlit then matched frame by frame with the models, asteroids and the starfield. This department also created cartoon

animated storyboards called animatics. While editing the live action sequences, the film editors used the animated storyboards to fill in special effects sequences which were to be added later. The animatics helped the editors to more easily envision the film in total, and were also useful in coordinating the pacing and timing of the effects shots.

Stunningly visual, the whole sequence is a prime example of the necessity to heighten reality when dealing with fantasy.

Composite shot of Millennium Falcon evading TIE fighters; Terry Chostner, airbrushing by Bob Jacobs and Ron Larson

1

2

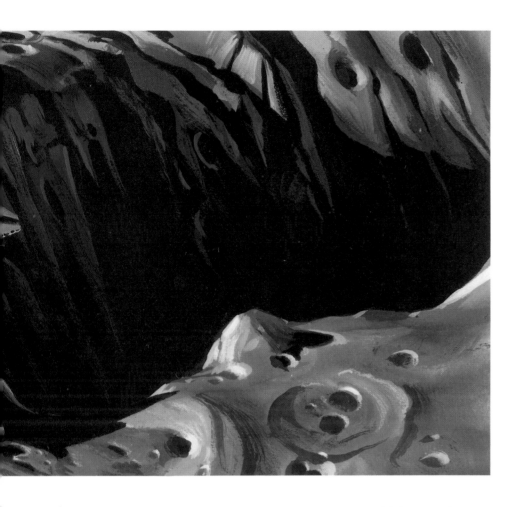

1
Production paintings,
Ralph McQuarrie;
The flaring explosions in this painting occur as asteroids collide in their movement through space. In the film excitement was added by having Han dodge through the narrow canyons and craters of an even larger asteroid. In his efforts to escape the ongoing asteroid storm, he discovers this cave.
2
After coming to rest in what they believe to be merely a great cave, the Rebels are startled to find the floor of the cave moving and the entrance growing smaller. They leap to the controls and fly through what turns out to be a gap in the teeth of a huge creature.

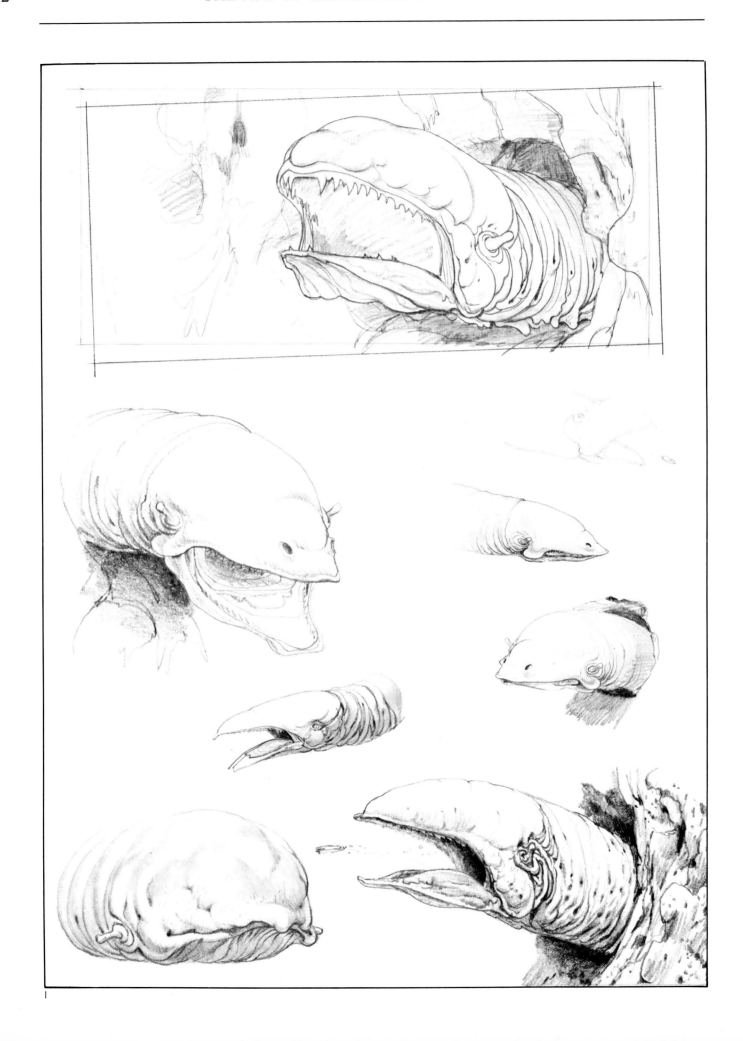

1
Sketches for space slug,
Ralph McQuarrie
2
Sketches for Mynocks,
Ralph McQuarrie

2

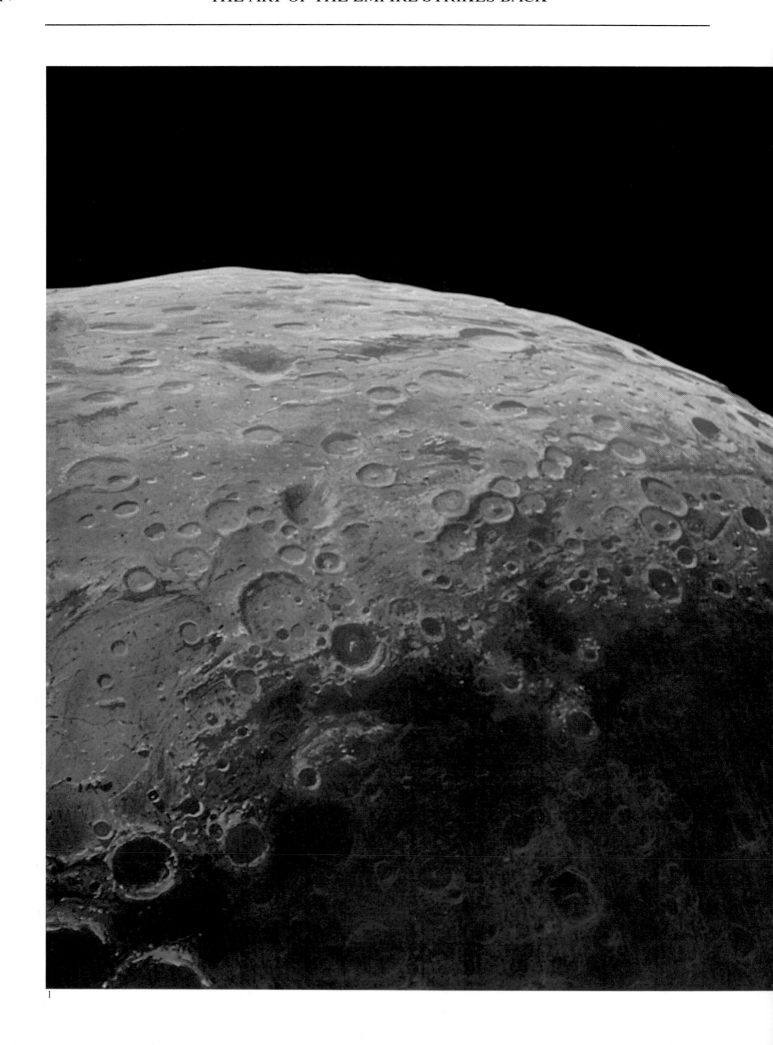

1

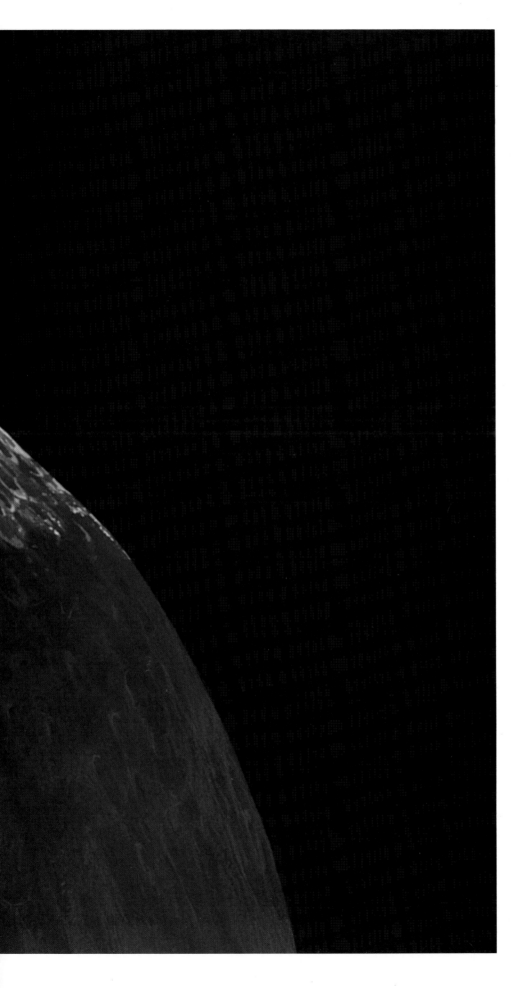

1
Matte painting of asteroid surface,
Mike Pangrazio

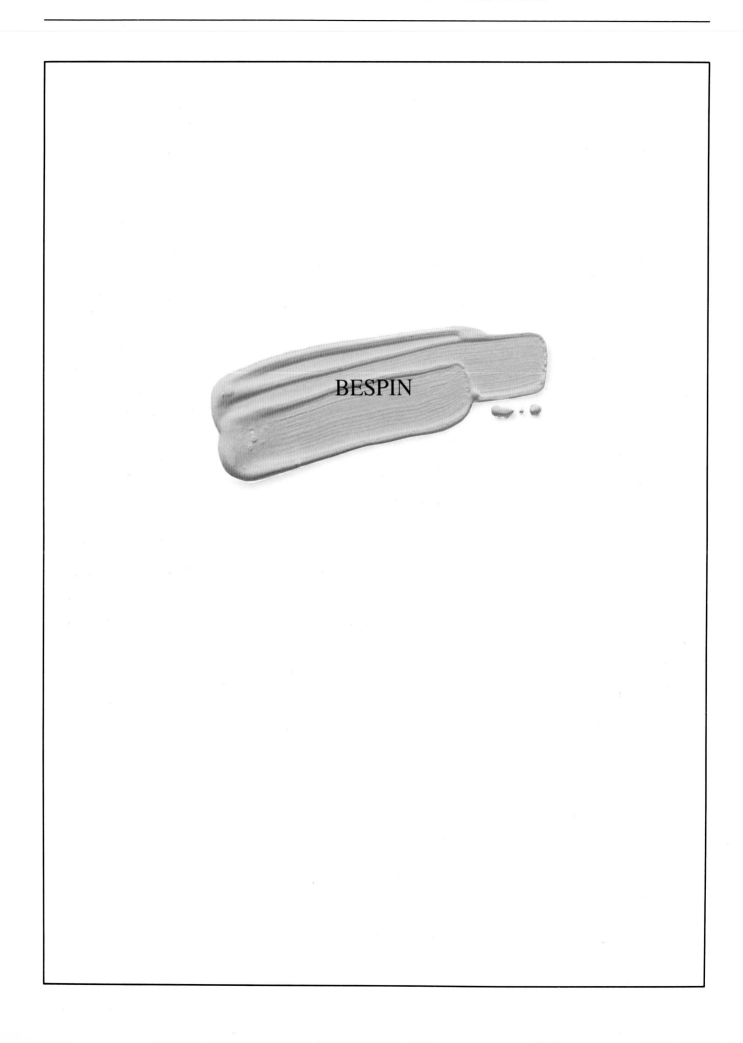

BESPIN

Bespin's wondrous Cloud City is one of the galaxy's major trading ports. It floats above the planet and rests upon a shaft which leads to a huge processing generator. Cloud City citizens are an industrious people whose advanced technology enables them to export the rare anti-gravitational tibanna gas. Governed by flamboyant, ex-soldier of fortune and former owner of the Millennium Falcon, Lando Calrissian, Cloud City remains a neutral colony. Han Solo retreats to the center of this bustling free market to harbor the malfunctioning Millennium Falcon. Han hopes that his old running partner, Lando, will provide sanctuary for Princess Leia and Chewbacca.

Ethereal as a painter's brush stroke, the concept of a floating city was first thought of as a possibility for an Imperial prison city in STAR WARS. This part of the story disappeared in a script rewrite but George Lucas liked the image very much so the floating city was held onto for use in THE EMPIRE STRIKES BACK.

It was difficult to make the scenes that take place in Cloud City believable. This difficulty was heightened by the fact that the viewing audience would know that such a location does not exist. Subconsciously they would register the fact that some trick had to be used. The challenge for the art department and the matte painters was to create a new world without disrupting the story's believability.

In THE EMPIRE STRIKES BACK, the Cloud City of Bespin has a circular, streamlined quality. This look predominates the city's architecture and vehicles. Extending this motif to the city's interior spaces, production designer Norman Reynolds wanted the reactor shaft sets to show the vertical, tubular structures that support the surface shapes. In the carbon-freezing chamber, Reynolds opened up the structures forming geometrical patterns. This theatrical setting became the stage for Luke's climactic duel against Darth Vader. Built twelve feet off the ground, the set allowed the camera to be positioned at dramatic angles for Han Solo's frozen interment and Luke's vengeful lightsaber duel.

The matte painting department at ILM is headed by veteran matte artist, Harrison Ellenshaw. Responsible for over eighty separate paintings in THE EMPIRE STRIKES BACK, Ellenshaw was assisted by design consultant, Ralph McQuarrie and Mike Pangrazio. This department was instrumental in the careful planning of the paintings. The desired effect was charted out in storyboards and the painters were responsible for keeping up with changes in location, character, and

composition of each particular shot.

A matte painting is, very simply, a painting done to blend with the photographic elements of a shot to make the final result look completely real. During this process the matte painter must communicate closely with the production designer since the paintings must convey the style of the sets. The most common technique used for matte painting is to have the subject matter painted on a piece of glass and have the live action projected onto a clear area. The two primary methods of projection used are front and rear. This technique can be best illustrated by using a scene from THE EMPIRE STRIKES BACK as an example: Han has just landed at the Cloud City landing platform and is greeted by Lando Calrissian. The actors appear in the live-action plate which was shot in England. The matte painting depicts the city's skyline at sunset. The live action is then projected onto a reflective screen which is the skyline painting. The combined image is then bounced back at a camera and

refilmed to make a final negative.

When a front projection process is used, the live-action plate cannot be moved. It must be refilmed in the exact frame position it had when originally shot. If the images don't match up the painting must be redone. The rear projection process allows for a little more freedom. Because of differences in the projector, the live-action plate can be reduced and repositioned to fit into the matte painting. The live action is projected from behind the painting onto a translucent material. The scene in which Princess Leia looks out over Cloud City from Lando's penthouse suite is a perfect example of the use of the rear projection technique.

When matte paintings are combined with live action and miniature effects in a front projection process called latent imaging, a different process is involved. Several exposures are made. One is developed while the others are kept in refrigeration. The developed film is examined to make sure the matte painting is aligned through the entire sequence. If all goes well, then the second exposure is developed and given to the animation department. This shot with the matte paintings and animation creates the final image. The other exposures, as a safety precaution, are stored for future use. When the film gets to the matte painting phase, the filmmaker realizes the potential of the live-action footage. It then becomes the task and challenge of the matte painter to make this potential a reality.

*Matte painting of Bespin,
Mike Pangrazio*

1

1
Production painting,
Ralph McQuarrie;
Buoyed above the clouds, this majestic city is bathed in golden sunlight. Once the headquarters of great leaders, the city's various levels represent all strata of society from the lowest mining Ugnaught to the highest royal official. Having grown at random, evidence of the city's glorious past is seen in the monumental structures which remain. The top level is reminiscent of the New York City skyline. The verandas along the sides are actually huge landing ports.

Joe Johnston designed the twin-pod cloud car, seen on the left amidst the dust clouds.

1

2

3

5

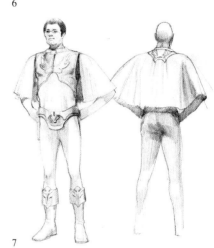

6

7

1-3, 7
Lando costume sketches,
Ralph McQuarrie
4
Production paintings,
Ralph McQuarrie;
A full scale replica of the Millennium
Falcon was built for scenes such as the
Rebels' escape from Cloud City. The
structure created many new angles from
which the cameraman could film the
live action. McQuarrie's production
painting was done as a matte study of
the city's towers and horizon.
5
Illuminated by northern lights, the
landing platform is located up in the
towers atop Cloud City. When the Mil-
lennium Falcon arrives, Han and Leia
are met by Lando and his aide. At the
time McQuarrie was doing this paint-
ing the character of the aide was not
yet developed and the figure of a
woman was chosen as a possibility.
6
Thumbnail sketches of
Rebels departure from Bespin,
Ralph McQuarrie

2

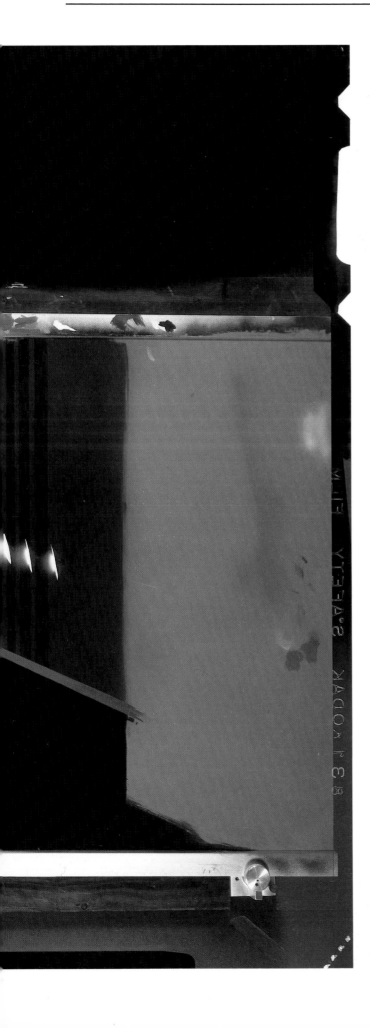

1
*Matte painting of Millennium Falcon
and Bespin landing port,
Ralph McQuarrie*
2
*Detail of matte painting with live-
action plate*

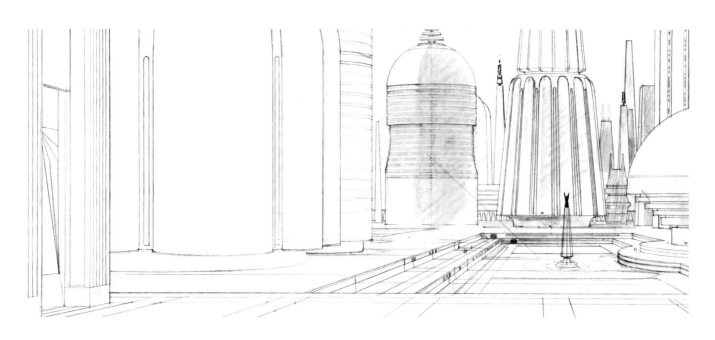

2

3

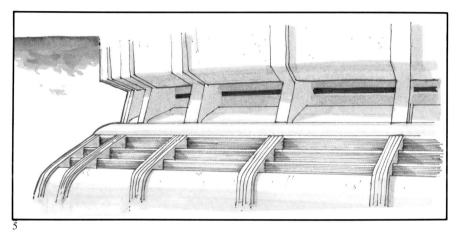

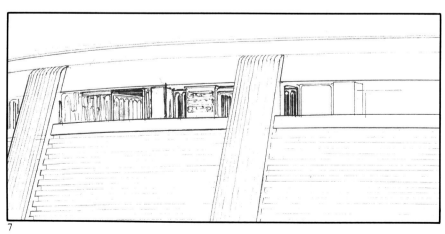

1, 2, 4, 6, 7
Sketches of Bespin architecture,
Ralph McQuarrie
3, 5
Bespin architecture, Joe Johnston

1

2

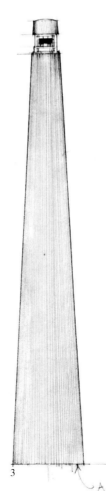

*Production paintings,
Ralph McQuarrie;
A study for a matte painting, this
picture was composed around the
window area which was to be filled in
with the live-action plate from England.
In the film, Princess Leia replaced
Han in this shot. The sky and clouds
were added in the matte process.
Photographed with a blue screen
background, the cloud cars move
across the sky.*
2
*Han and Leia become suspicious of
Lando's gracious hospitality when
Chewbacca returns to their guest penthouse with a damaged See-Threepio.
This room was described as being sun-
filled and central to four or five adjoining apartments. McQuarrie wanted to
project the feeling of a comfortable,
luxurious space. He gave the room a
sunken area surrounded with couches,
then added columns and metal framed
sliding doors that operate without
touch.*

*The design for the apartment set seen
in THE EMPIRE STRIKES BACK was
re-designed by production designer
Norman Reynolds.*
3
*Construction drawing for Cloud City
towers, Michael Boone under the
direction of Norman Reynolds*

1
*Matte painting of Bespin skyline,
Mike Pangrazio*

2
*Detail of matte painting with live-
action plate*

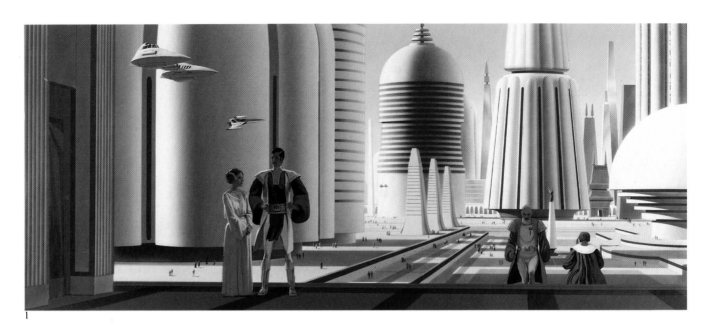

1

2

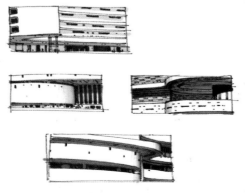

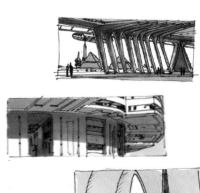

3

Cloud City / modelbuilders note: sculpture and landing platform...
035f
©ILM '79

Cloud City / main concourse
0358
©ILM '79

4

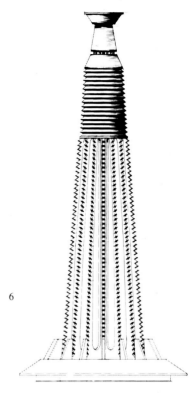

6

5

1
*Production painting,
Ralph McQuarrie;*
*Lando stands proudly as Princess Leia
looks out over the cityscape. McQuarrie gave the upper deck of Cloud City a
cool, futuristic look. The smooth and
massive sculptured surfaces were inspired by the art deco movement of the
1920's. The round shapes of Bespin's
architecture set it apart from the angu-
lar shapes that make up most cities
we know.*

*This area of the city contains the ad-
ministrative buildings and the monuments to past great leaders. Figures are
shown coming and going on a broad
staircase leading down to a vast square
crossed in places by moving walkways.
A stickler for detail, McQuarrie even
gave the distant pedestrians shadows.*
2, 4
*Sketches of Bespin architecture,
Joe Johnston*
3
*Thumbnail sketches of Bespin
architecture, Ralph McQuarrie*
5
*Sketches of Bespin monuments,
Ralph McQuarrie*
6
*Bespin monument,
Richard Dawking under the
direction of Norman Reynolds*

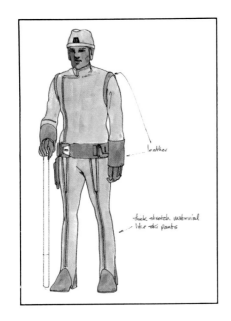

leather

thick stretch material like ski pants

Princess cloud city

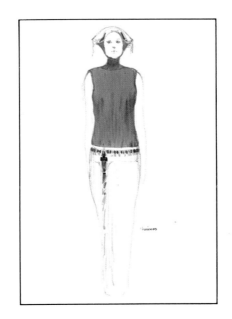

Princess

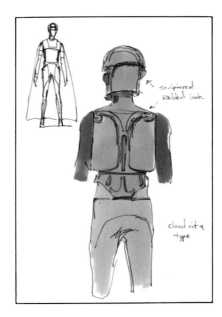

sculptured padded look

cloud city type

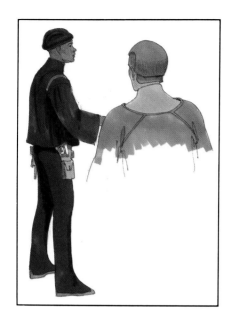

Costume sketches of Bespin citizens,
Ralph McQuarrie

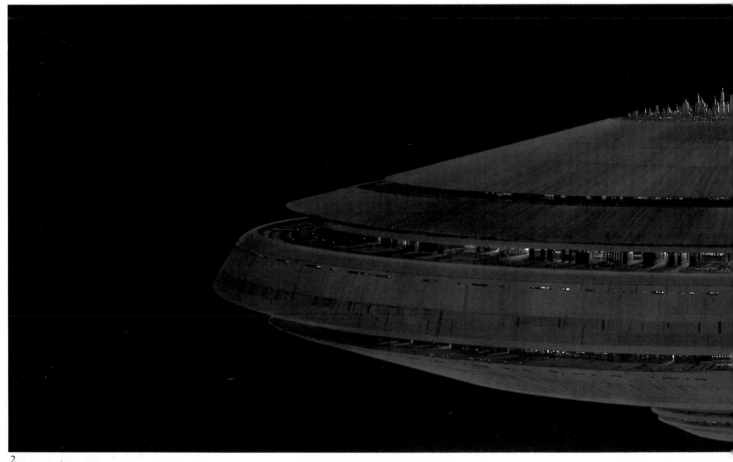

2

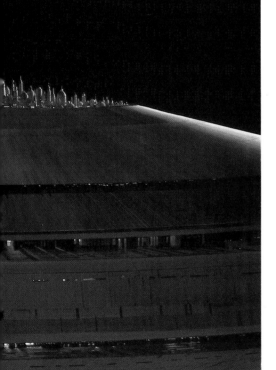

1
Matte painting of Bespin horizon,
Harrison Ellenshaw
2
Matte painting of Cloud City,
Ralph McQuarrie
3
Thumbnail sketches for bi-pod cars,
Ralph McQuarrie

3

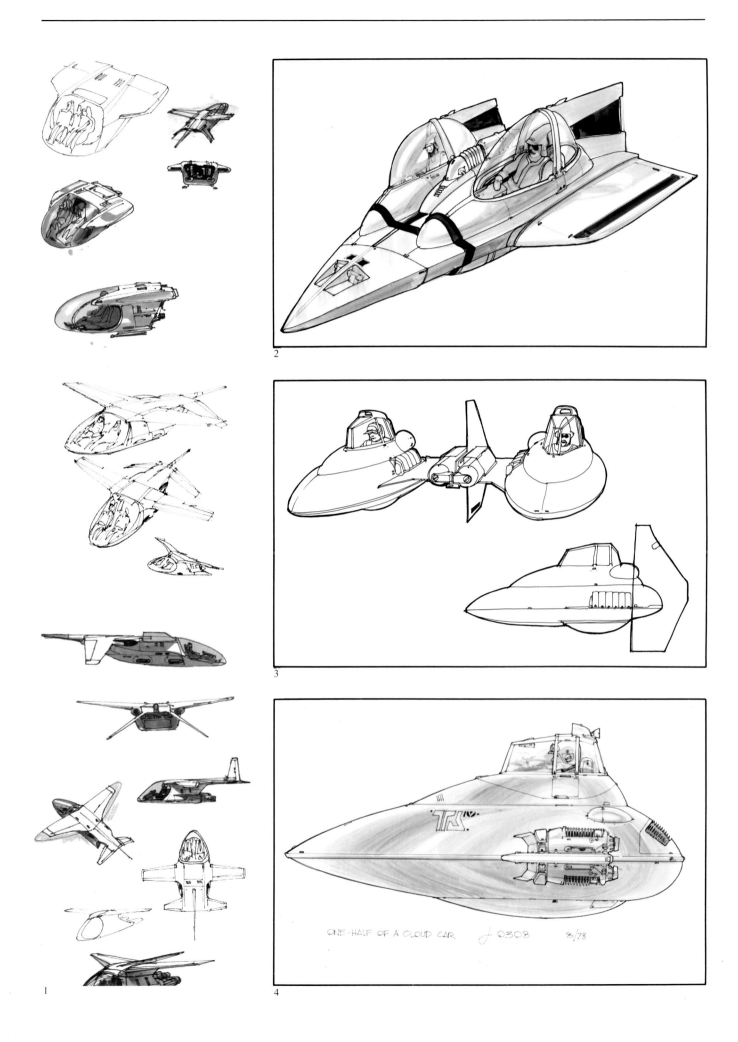

One-half of a cloud car.   0308   8/78

5

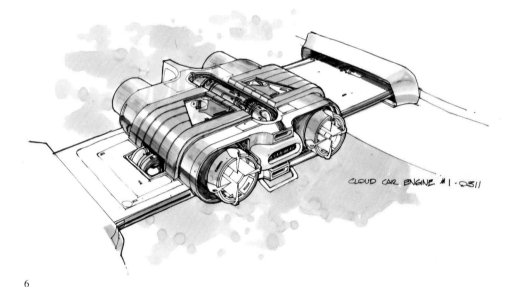

CLOUD CAR ENGINE #1-0511

6

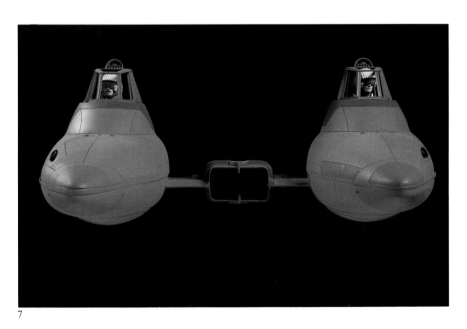

7

1
Thumbnail sketches for bi-pod cars,
Ralph McQuarrie
2 - 4
Sketches for bi-pod cars, Joe Johnston
5, 7
Side and front view of bi-pod
car models, photographs by
Terry Chostner
6
Bi-pod car engine, Joe Johnston

2

1

3

4

1, 4
Lando costume sketches,
Ralph McQuarrie
2
Production paintings,
Ralph McQuarrie;
This hall is based on a sketch from a series done to establish Cloud City architecture. It is high among the towers of the city. Clouds and other towers can be seen through the windows on either side. It is designed to inspire awe in those visiting dignitaries who are led through it on their way to meetings with officials of the city. The dining table was added when the room was deemed suitable for the first meeting in Cloud City between Darth Vader and our heroes. Vader, using the Force, will soon snatch Han's pistol from him and take the Rebels as prisoners.

In the film, the actual set was built from a different concept by Production Designer Norman Reynolds.
3
Han, now held in detention, has just come down the elevator to the prison area. Unable to see out of the elevator, Han does not know that Boba Fett and Lando have been bargaining with the Dark Lord over his fate. Warrior Boba Fett's caped costume is medieval in design. To the left, a creature-prisoner antagonizes a guard. Light emanating from the top of the shaft focuses our attention on Han. The bars of the elevator cast shadows out into the room thus heightening the dramatic effect of the scene. The doors, resembling old juke boxes, lead to the prison cells and the slots under the doors allow trays to be slid in to the unseen prisoners.

This design was not used in the film.

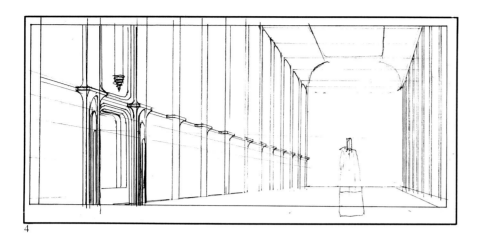

4

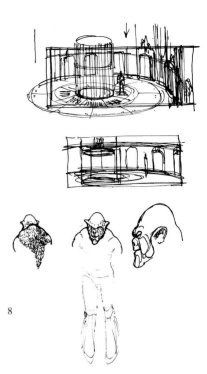

5

8

6

9

7

1-4
*Sketches of Bespin dining hall and
hallways, Ralph McQuarrie*
5, 6
*Sketches of prison detention area,
Ralph McQuarrie*
7
*Prison detention area,
Norman Reynolds*
8
*Sketch of prison detention area and
prisoners, Ralph McQuarrie*
9
*Early sketch of Lando,
Ralph McQuarrie*

1

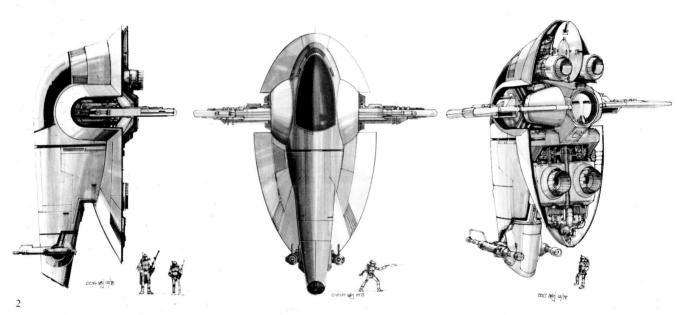

2

1
*To depict one of Bespin's many hall-
ways, McQuarrie chose the moment
when Princess Leia and Chewbacca
fire their lasers through broken glass at
Boba Fett's departing ship. See-Threepio peeks out from the elevator, not
quite ready for another fight. The appearance of Artoo-Detoo signals that
Luke has arrived on the Cloud City.*

*This action took place on the landing
platform instead of the hallway in the
film.*

2
*Three views of Boba Fett's ship,
Slave I, Nilo Rodis-Jamero*

3
*Slave I model,
photographs by Terry Chostner*

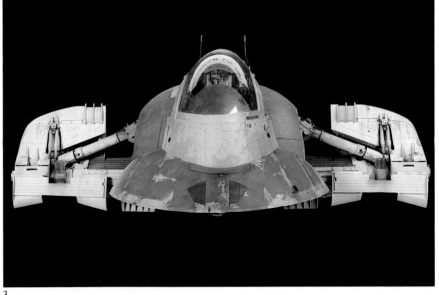

3

1

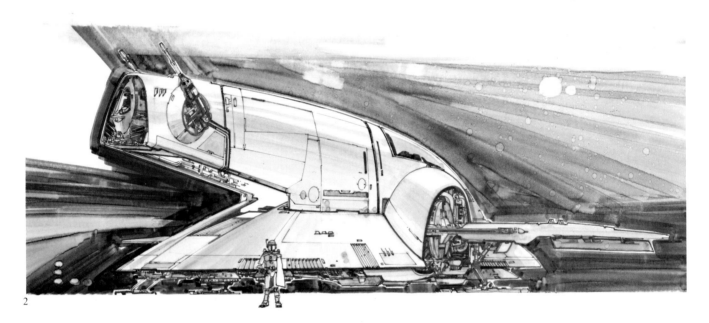

2

1
Matte painting of Bespin landing port
with Slave I model, Harrison Ellenshaw

2
Sketch of Slave I on landing port,
Nilo Rodis-Jamero

3
Interior of Boba Fett's ship,
Nilo Rodis-Jamero

4, 5, 12, 13
Boba Fett helmet and costume
concepts, Ralph McQuarrie

6-11
Boba Fett helmet concepts,
Joe Johnston

4 ◀
Slave I model in flying position,
photographed by Terry Chostner,
retouched by Harrison Ellenshaw

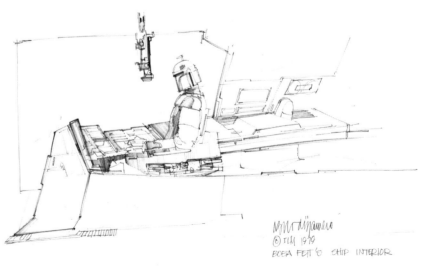

3

4

5

6

7

8

9

10

11

12

13

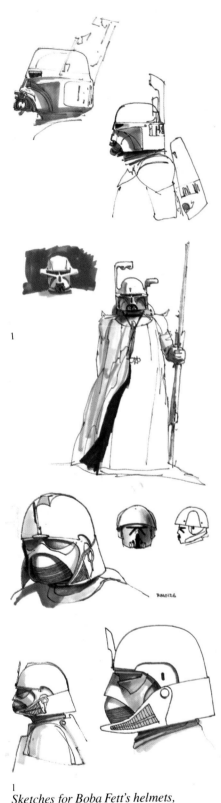

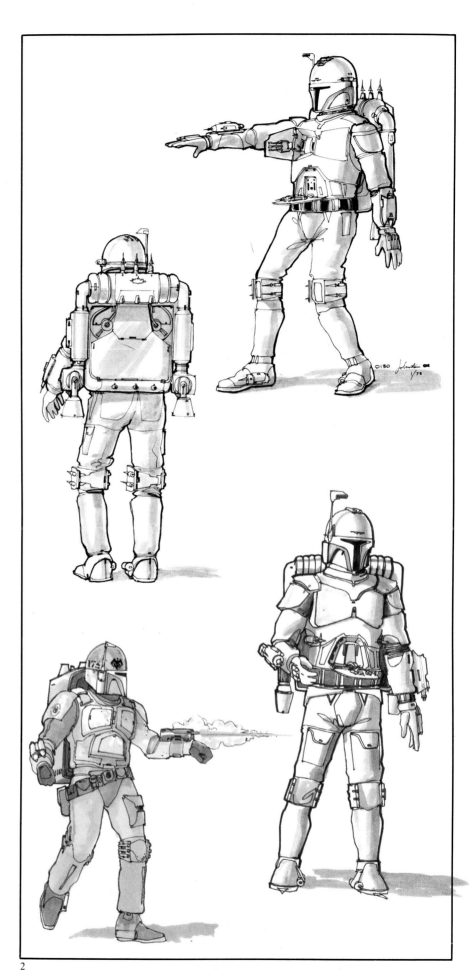

1
Sketches for Boba Fett's helmets,
Ralph McQuarrie
2
Sketches of Boba Fett, Joe Johnston
3
Boba Fett in action with sketches
of fellow bounty hunters. Sketches by
Ralph McQuarrie, photograph by
Bob Seidemann, airbrushing by
Ron Larson

2

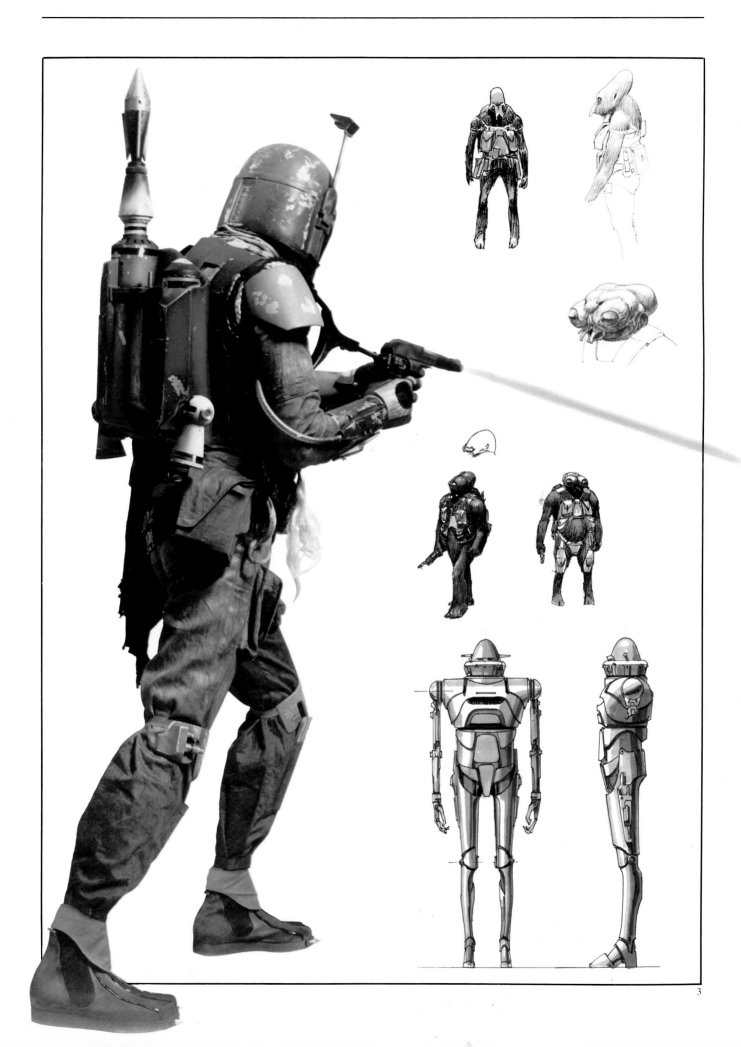

1

2

4

3

1, 2
Production paintings,
Ralph McQuarrie;
The carbon-freezing chamber is lo-
cated deep in the city near the reactor
shaft. Above is an early concept of the
stage on which Han is entombed to be
given as human cargo to bounty hunter
Boba Fett. A cold, blue light illumi-
nates vapor coming from the freezing
chamber below. High above are rails to
carry the carbon ladle and the great
claw which lifts the metal encapsulated
frozen life forms from the pit. The
trenches and foil forms of equipment
in the room were designed to provide
a place for the cliff-hanging duel
between Vader and Skywalker.

Later in production, designer Norman
Reynolds opened up the space to allow
for more dramatic possibilities for the
duel between Vader and Luke. Over-
head is an apparatus that is capable of
focusing a ray onto the platform.
McQuarrie painted this version of the
carbon-freezing chamber which
closely resembles the stage seen in
the film.

3, 4
Sketches for Ugnaughts,
Ralph McQuarrie

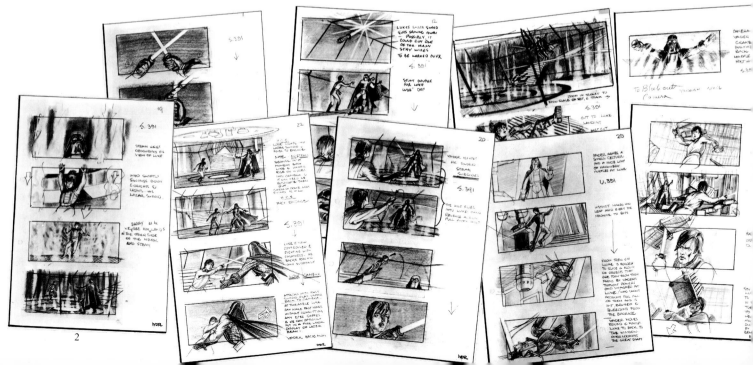

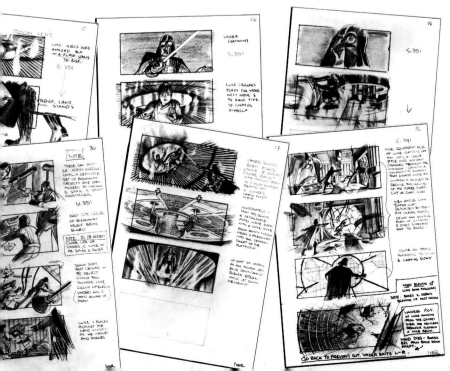

1
Production painting,
Ralph McQuarrie;
Enclosed in the spider-web structure of
the carbon-freezing chamber, Luke
Skywalker and Darth Vader duel. The
room is located within one of the many
vanes in the reactor shaft.
2
Storyboards of duel, Ivor Beddoes

1

2

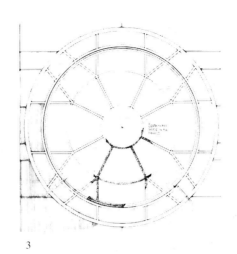

3

1
Production paintings,
Ralph McQuarrie;
This visualizes the moment before
Vader, using the Force, hurls a heavy
piece of equipment at Luke. As the
equipment smashes the round viewport
behind Luke, he is sucked out the win-
dow by a rush of air coming up the
reactor shaft. Through the window we
see the opposite shaft wall a half mile
or so away. The small lights are actu-
ally large ports for landing shuttle craft
travelling in the shaft.
2
The rudderlike vanes of the reactor
shaft are used to create desired changes
in airflow which control the city's
movements in space and route gases to
be processed. The shaft is about a mile
in diameter and is a structure which
houses a number of facilities related to
the manufacturing and processing of
tibanna gas.
3
Elevation of reactor control room
window, Michael Boone under the
direction of Norman Reynolds

1

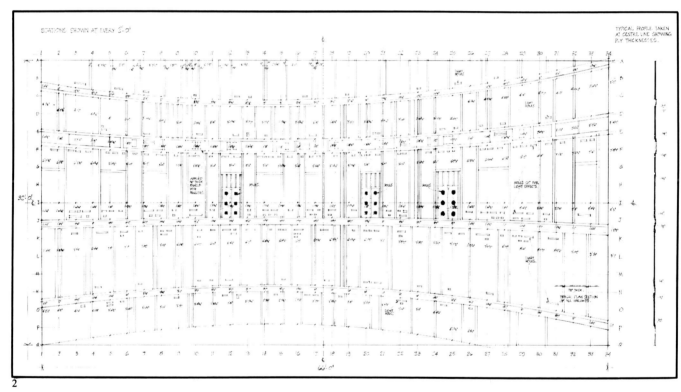

2

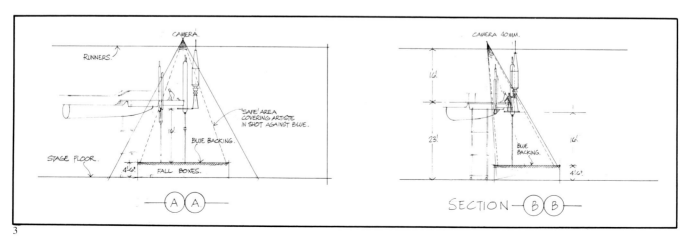

3

4

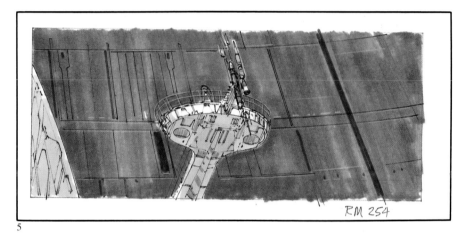

5

6

7

1
Production painting,
Ralph McQuarrie;
On the vanes' edges, projecting into the
center of the shaft, their cantileveral
platforms can be seen. These platforms
hold delicate measuring devices that
monitor the changes in pressure and
the types of gases in the shaft. The
whole complex provides the location
for a duel between Luke Skywalker and
Darth Vader.
2
Construction drawing of reactor
shaft wall and landing ports,
Ted Ambrose under the direction of
Norman Reynolds
3
Drawing for camera angle set-up of
landing port, Ted Ambrose under the
direction of Norman Reynolds
4-7
Sketches of reactor shaft locations,
Ralph McQuarrie
1 ▶
Matte painting of reactor shaft,
Harrison Ellenshaw
2-4 ▶
Matte painting of reactor shaft gantry,
Ralph McQuarrie

1

2

3

4

1

1
*Matte painting of exterior Bespin
reactor shaft, Harrison Ellenshaw*

1

1
Production painting,
Ralph McQuarrie;
During the laser duel, Luke falls from
the vane platform and is then sucked
into an air shaft which leads to this
exhaust port on the underside of the
city. This painting served to establish a
possible design for the port and for the
fragile antennalike device which Luke
is able to grasp long enough for the
Millennium Falcon to swing past and
rescue him.
2
Camera angle set-up of Luke hanging
in reactor shaft, Ted Ambrose under the
direction of Norman Reynolds

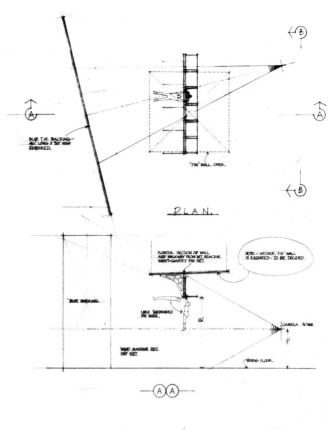

PLAN.

A A

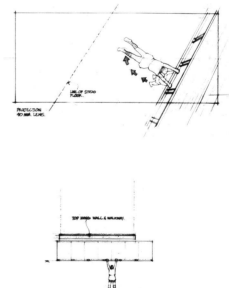

2

B B

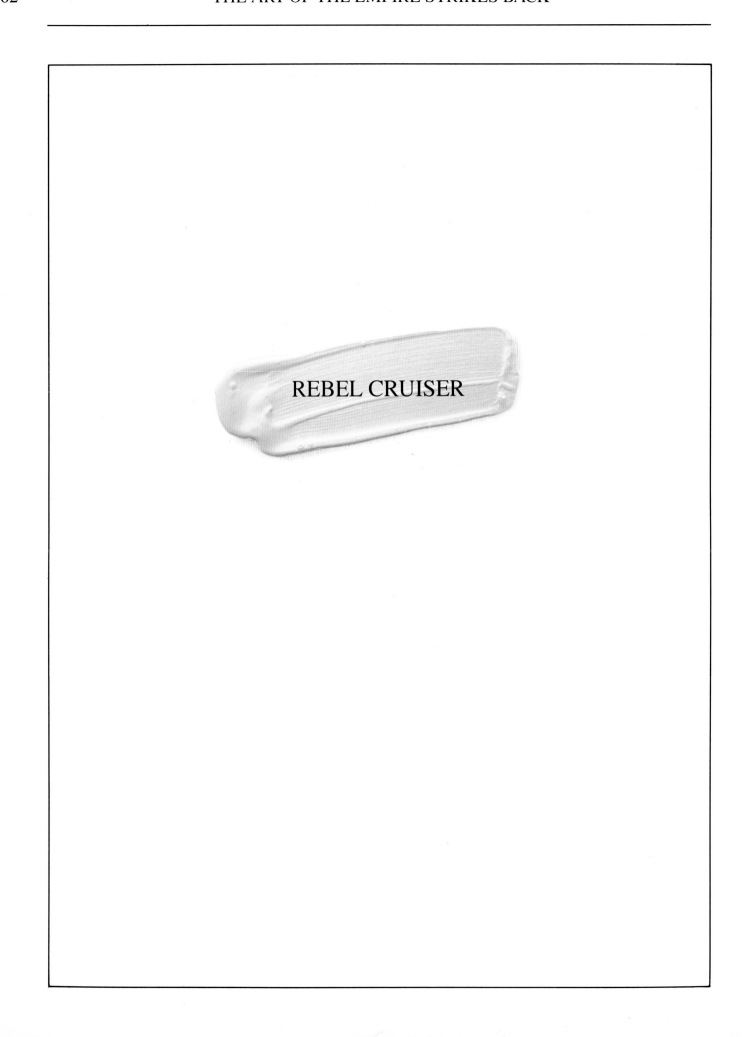

REBEL CRUISER

A Rebel Star Cruiser drifts in deep space at the Rebel rendezvous far away from any inhabitable planetary systems. Here, Princess Leia tends the wounds of Luke Skywalker during the short time in which the Rebels must plan their next course of action.

Each phase in the development of THE EMPIRE STRIKES BACK had decisive moments of spontaneous creation which enhanced the reality of the film. An example of this was the final design of the Rebel Star Cruiser

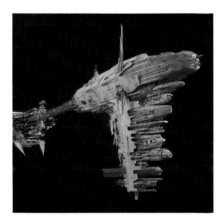

which did not change very much from the preliminary sketches done by Joe Johnston and Nilo Rodis-Jamero. When placed in front of the camera, the model's free-flowing form had a remarkable depth of field. Dennis Muren, lighting designer for all mattes and models, found that the fluid mechanical quality of the ship lent itself well to lighting. The Rebel Cruiser was one of the last models to be constructed.

When an idea captures the imagination of the people the way the STAR WARS saga has, it is evident that man's primal dream to explore and inhabit the universe has become a conscious longing. One day soon, in a reality not so far away, it is hoped that the nations of our world may collectively unite and reach for the stars.

MAY THE FORCE BE WITH YOU

Rebel Cruiser model, photograph by Terry Chostner

1

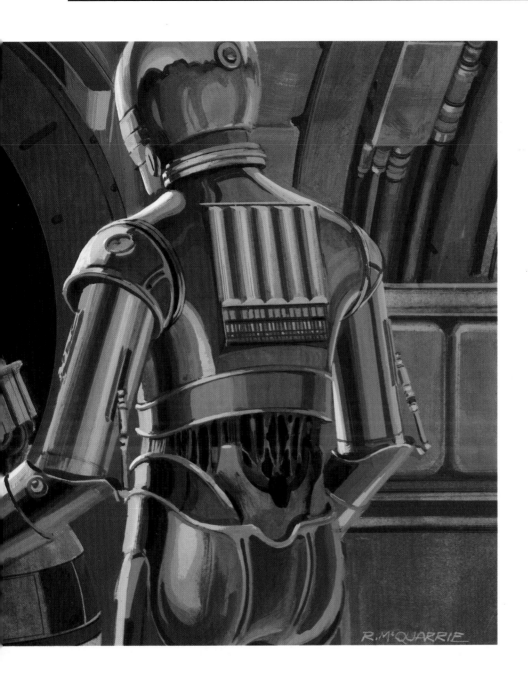

1
Production painting,
Ralph McQuarrie;
A moment of tender kinship in the
medical bay, See-Threepio and Artoo-
Detoo watch as surgical droid Too-
Onebee operates on the young Jedi's
wound. McQuarrie envisioned Too-
Onebee's medical staff as including an
assortment of support computers. The
unit at the foot of the bed is connected
to Luke's arm and functions as anesthe-
siologist while the optical unit over-
head gives the attending surgeon a
second view from which to make
decisions and a third hand for the
more intricate procedures.

1

2

3

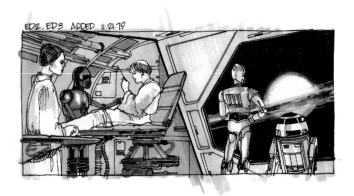

1

1
Storyboards, Nilo Rodis-Jamero

1, 2 ◄
Rebel Cruiser model,
photograph by Terry Chostner

3 ◄
Rebel Cruiser with live-action plate,
photograph by Terry Chostner

ED4, ED6, ED8 ADDED 11·21·79

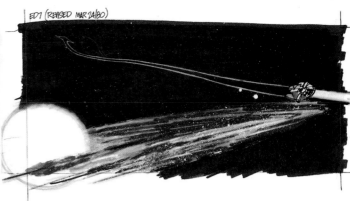

ED7 (REVISED MAR 24/80)

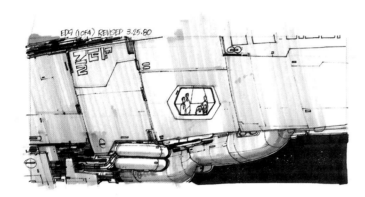

ED9 (1OF4) REVISED 3·25·80

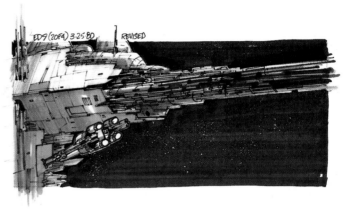

ED9 (2OF4) 3·25·80   REVISED

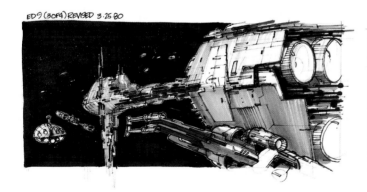

ED9 (3OF4) REVISED 3·25·80

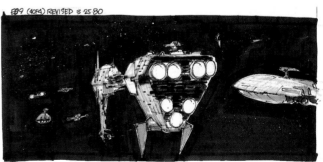

ED9 (4OF4) REVISED 3·25·80

1

1
Production painting,
Ralph McQuarrie;
This painting was done with the final
scene of the film in mind. Luke and
Leia look out a round window of the
Rebel Cruiser as the Millennium
Falcon, piloted by Lando Calrissian,
goes off in pursuit of Boba Fett.

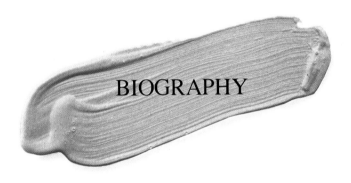

BIOGRAPHY

RALPH McQUARRIE, Design Consultant and Conceptual Artist, studied at Art Center College of Design in Los Angeles and began work as an illustrator for the Boeing Company, Litton Industries, and Kaiser Graphics as well as CBS News. McQuarrie's interpretations of Apollo space missions gave millions of television viewers an accurate idea of what was happening out in space. George Lucas learned of McQuarrie in late 1975 and, very soon after, Ralph was at work on production paintings for STAR WARS. His other credits include CLOSE ENCOUNTERS OF THE THIRD KIND and BATTLESTAR GALACTICA.

PHIL TIPPETT, Stop Motion Animation, graduated from U.C. Irvine with a degree in Fine Arts. He then became commercial business partners with fellow Stop Motion Animator, Jon Berg. Both men continually contribute to the state of the art. His film credits include, an extensive list of commercials, STAR WARS, PIRANHA and now THE EMPIRE STRIKES BACK.

JOE JOHNSTON, Art Director—Visual Effects, is a transplanted Texan, who studied oceanography at Pasadena City College before enrolling in the industrial design program at Cal State Long Beach. Before joining the STAR WARS team as a storyboard artist in 1975, he worked on two science fiction made-for-T.V. movies, a remake of H.G. Wells' "WAR OF THE WORLDS" and "STAR WATCH." During the interim between STAR WARS and starting his work on THE EMPIRE STRIKES BACK, he did many of the designs for BATTLESTAR GALACTICA. An interpreter of ideas, he is an integral part of the ILM staff.

JON BERG, Stop Motion Animation, studied Photography and Fine Arts at Santa Monica City College before accumulating an impressive list of commercial credits as a Stop Motion Animator. Starting his film career with STAR WARS, he has since worked on the horror film, PIRANHA, and has been busy since 1978 working on THE EMPIRE STRIKES BACK.

NILO RODIS-JAMERO, Assistant Art Director—Visual Effects, new to the film world, studied Industrial Design at San Jose State before going to work for General Motors' Advanced Experimental Design Center. He then worked for two years as a Design Consultant on boat and aircraft interiors. His last job before joining Lucasfilm was for the F.M.C. Corporation, designing heavy industrial vehicles and military tanks. At ILM he collaborated with Joe Johnston on many of the craft in THE EMPIRE STRIKES BACK.

RICHARD EDLUND, Special Visual Effects, attended film school at the University of Southern California and the U.S. Navy Photographic School. His film credits include STAR WARS, CHINA SYNDROME, BATTLESTAR GALACTICA and various television programs and logos.

BRUCE NICHOLSON, Optical Photography Supervisor, was a Social Science major at University of California at Berkeley and went on to study film at Sherwood Oaks and U.C.L.A. He is now head of the ILM Optical Department. His film credits include STAR WARS, CLOSE ENCOUNTERS OF THE THIRD KIND, and BATTLESTAR GALACTICA.

NORMAN REYNOLDS, Production Designer, completed two years of national service in the RAF then entered the film industry as a draftsman in 1962. An ardent film lover, he worked his way up over the next ten years on such films as THUNDERBALL, KELLY'S HEROES and A WARM DECEMBER. This led to a prestigious career as Art Director on the films PHASE IV, THE LITTLE PRINCE, THE INCREDIBLE SARAH, LUCKY LADY, STAR WARS and SUPERMAN. Production Designer on THE EMPIRE STRIKES BACK, he will continue in this role for the George Lucas and Steven Spielberg collaboration of RAIDERS OF THE LOST ARK.

PETER KURAN, Animation and Rotoscope Supervisor, studied film graphics, animation and optical printing at California Institute of the Arts in Valencia and learned about special effects and optical printing on a special one year program at Disney Studios. An animator on STAR WARS, Kuran's other credits include BATTLESTAR GALACTICA, PIRANHA , AIRPLANE plus numerous low-budget features and commercials.

DENNIS MUREN, Effects Director of Photography, graduated from Cal State in Los Angeles with a degree in Business Advertising. His film credits include STAR WARS, CLOSE ENCOUNTERS OF THE THIRD KIND, WILLIE WONKA, BATTLESTAR GALACTICA, and various space education films and commercials.

JOHN MOLLO, Costume Designer, has written and illustrated six books on military costume. His widely hailed MILITARY FASHION 1640-1914 is a classic text on the subject. Entering the motion picture industry as a technical advisor on Tony Richardson's THE CHARGE OF THE LIGHT BRIGADE, he continued in this capacity on THE ADVENTURES OF GERARD, NICHOLAS AND ALEXANDRA and BARRY LYNDON. STAR WARS marked his debut as a costume designer.

STUART FREEBORN, Make-up and Special Creature Designer, began work as a make-up artist for Alexander Korda in 1936. He has worked on such notable films as THE THIEF OF BAGHDAD , OLIVER TWIST and THE BRIDGE OVER THE RIVER KWAI. A prolific artist, he is known for his make-up for the three Peter Sellers characters in DR. STRANGELOVE, the apes in Stanley Kubrick's 2001, and the now famous cantina sequence in STAR WARS. His recent credits include THE WIND AND THE LION, MURDER ON THE ORIENT EXPRESS, SUPERMAN and THE EMPIRE STRIKES BACK. He has just completed work on SUPERMAN II.

HARRISON ELLENSHAW, Matte Painting Supervisor, is an expert matte painter and has produced some of filmdom's most wondrous backgrounds. After majoring in Psychology at Whittier College he went on to work on STAR WARS, THE BLACK HOLE, BIG WEDNESDAY, THE MAN WHO FELL TO EARTH and PETE'S DRAGON.

LORNE PETERSON, Chief Model Maker, is the head of the ILM Model Shop and has a degree in Fine Arts from Long Beach State University in California. Specializing in science-oriented adventures, his credits include STAR WARS, CHINA SYNDROME, CLOSE ENCOUNTERS OF THE THIRD KIND, SPACE ACADEMY and BATTLESTAR GALACTICA.

BRIAN JOHNSON, Special Visual Effects, attended a public school in Great Britain and then served in the RAF for two years. Now a general in the ranks of cinema, a partial list of his credits include work on ALIEN, REVENGE OF THE PINK PANTHER, MEDUSA TOUCH, SPACE 1999, GLITTER BALL, TAMARIND, and THE EMPIRE STRIKES BACK.

MIKE PANGRAZIO, Matte Artist, started his film career right after graduating from Hoover High in Glendale, California. Having worked on television's MAN FROM ATLANTIS and BATTLESTAR GALACTICA, his work is now prominently displayed in THE EMPIRE STRIKES BACK.

IVOR BEDDOES, Sketch Artist, spent many years in the theatre as a choreographer, dancer, costume and set designer, and actor. He began his film career as a sketch artist on THE RED SHOES. As a sketch artist and matte painter he now has over fifty films to his credit including CLEOPATRA, DIAMONDS ARE FOREVER, THE SPY WHO LOVED ME, DR. STRANGELOVE, CASINO ROYALE, SLEUTH, THE SEVEN PERCENT SOLUTION, THE YELLOW ROLLS ROYCE, A SHOT IN THE DARK, SUPERMAN I and II, STAR WARS and THE EMPIRE STRIKES BACK.

THE EMPIRE STRIKES BACK

The *Millennium Falcon* on the
Cloud City landing platform.
Production art duplicating
camera angle of original film;
George Hull.

There are many celestial wonders in the STAR WARS universe, from the desert wastelands of Tatooine explored in A NEW HOPE to the cool forests of Endor seen in RETURN OF THE JEDI. But of all the trilogy chapters, THE EMPIRE STRIKES BACK arguably offers the

most entrancing and spectacular sights, among them the ice planet of Hoth, the swampy jungles of Dagobah, and Cloud City floating above the giant planet Bespin.

These visions of EMPIRE were originally created using a variety of production techniques. Since Dagobah was scripted for extended scenes with Luke and Yoda, that environment was built on a huge soundstage at Elstree Studios in England, and featured a three-foot-deep lagoon accommodating a full-scale replica of Luke's crashed X-wing fighter, forty-foot-tall banyan trees built out of tubular steel and plaster, and truckloads of vines used to dress out the set.

For the Rebel snowspeeders and Imperial walkers battling on Hoth and for the exotic vistas of Cloud City, George Lucas' Industrial Light and Magic (ILM) visual effects artists took over. The Battle of

Storyboard image of Han Solo riding a tauntaun across the frozen wastes of Hoth in search of Luke Skywalker; George Hull.

Hoth sequence was produced as an optical composite effect that blended miniature models and sets with live-action footage, Cloud City was rendered with oil and brush matte paintings that combined live-action elements using in-camera techniques, thus bypassing the laborious optical printing process. Through the use of "front projection," live-action was literally projected onto a glass painted scene, and the camera — placed on the same side as the projector—recorded the resulting composite image.

By JEDI, the task of conjuring up an entire universe was already straining the limits of available technology. Despite the optical artist's superb technique and all the tricks of the trade that could be called upon to improve the filmed elements that moviemakers assembled and composited, optical effects were still restricted by the materials at hand in 1983.

Today, digital technology has transformed the art of cinematic storytelling, providing moviemakers with creative freedoms once only dreamed of. The touch of a brush stroke on a glass canvas has been largely replaced by 3-D paint systems and image processing tools. Models, creature effects, and even entire environments can now be constructed as three-dimensional, computer graphic (CG) effects, and a virtual camera can move with complete freedom through the digital realm. Elements can be easily digitized and seamlessly composited and manipulated to the cutting edge of a pixel point.

Digital tools at hand and with the twentieth anniversary of A NEW HOPE coming up in 1997, creator George Lucas saw an opportunity to not only theatrically rerelease his classic film, but to use the computer to finally address the problems originally foisted upon him by the limits of technology and lack of time and money. Lucas always wished he could have enlarged the scope of the spaceport town of Mos Eisley, breathed more life into the dewbacks ridden by stormtrooper patrols, and been able to create a convincing Jabba the Hutt for a pivotal encounter with Han Solo—using footage that ended up on the cutting room floor.

So in 1996, ILM was assigned to prepare the STAR WARS TRILOGY SPECIAL EDITION, and a 150-person-strong team tackled the specific shots on Lucas' wish list. Pacific Title was brought in to use traditional photochemical technology to recomposite some of the original opticals, YCM Labs provided color timings, and consultant Leon Briggs helped supervise the vital film restoration work on the original negative (from which the birthday prints would be struck). By early 1996, the major work had been completed on A NEW HOPE and was deemed so successful it was decided to apply special edition magic to THE EMPIRE STRIKES BACK and RETURN OF THE JEDI.

Thus, 1997 would mark a back-to-back rerelease of the entire saga. "We decided to just go for it and make this an event that celebrated the entire universe," noted Lucasfilm producer Rick McCallum, who headed up the project.

EMPIRE and JEDI would follow the same ground rules established during NEW HOPE work. "I think the most wonderful aspect of the Special Editions was that George only fixed things he couldn't do at the time," McCallum explained. "The notion was pure, it's not like things were being changed or added. And with digital technology, there's now a palette in which you can do whatever you want to."

As it turned out, it wasn't only George Lucas who wanted another crack at the classic STAR WARS films. ILM veteran Tom Rosseter, who joined the effects company in 1979 to work on optical lineup for EMPIRE, was one of those who had also dreamed about returning to the original work. "You know what they say, 'Be careful what you wish for because you might get it,'" said Rosseter, whose compositing expertise spans both traditional opticals and digital technology. "I'd always felt I could do everything better on EMPIRE if given the time, that I'd like to go back not just because of the new tools, but because with experience you develop skills to solve problems. At the time we were making EMPIRE, there were only a few people with extensive experience at that level of visual effects, and we were also building equipment and the company"—literally, construction of the ILM facility in Marin County, California.

There would be some 160 Special Edition shots for EMPIRE, most concentrated on enhancing the Cloud City sequence and providing digital fixes, notably on shots that displayed obvious matte lines and other revealing opticals. As always, the integrity of the original film would be maintained. For example, even though the lumbering walkers, those four-legged Imperial combat vehicles seen in the Battle of Hoth, had originally been created with stop-motion animation, and sometimes betrayed the

Far left: In the wampa's lair. This scene of the fearsome ice creature feasting on tauntaun remains was created the traditional way—with a set and a man in a creature suit. Still from film.

Left: The wampa, ice creature of Hoth; close-up of original puppet head. Still from film.

Below: Storyboards of the wampa; George Hull.

Below, left: Tilt-up shot on the wampa; George Hull.

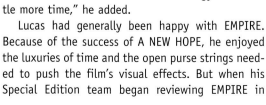

occasional pop or jitter endemic to the medium, the effect still represented the state-of-the-art of the day and would not be replaced by computer graphics recreations. "Our purpose in the Special Edition work was not to change the nature of a shot or rethink its choreography," noted Dave Carson, who had begun his ILM career on the original THE EMPIRE STRIKES BACK. Carson was visual effects supervisor for the EMPIRE and JEDI Special Editions. "We only wanted to change what would have been changed at the time if there'd been the same technology and a little more time," he added.

Lucas had generally been happy with EMPIRE. Because of the success of A NEW HOPE, he enjoyed the luxuries of time and the open purse strings needed to push the film's visual effects. But when his Special Edition team began reviewing EMPIRE in

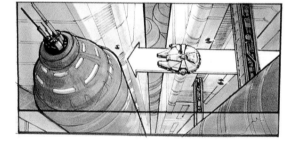

Top and middle, left: Storyboards of the *Millennium Falcon* approaching the floating Cloud City of Bespin; George Hull.

Right: Storyboard sequence of *Falcon* fly-through; George Hull.

ILM's high-tech screening room, problems literally loomed larger than life. Of particular concern was the famed Battle of Hoth, which, with its brightly lit snowfield battleground, sometimes betrayed telltale matte lines (unlike the optical composites in A NEW HOPE, where the blackness of space often hid the matte line around a spaceship element). Removing the distracting matte lines was deemed vital to retaining the feeling of awe and excitement remembered by fans of the initial theatrical release, and would ensure the theatrical impact for a new generation of effects-savvy moviegoers.

In many ways, the Special Edition effort was a time-traveling experience. The project team was literally delving into the alchemy of the "ancient" chemical baths and the limitations of optical compositing techniques. "It's just amazing that they [the optical department] were able to get the quality of work that most of the film has," Carson com-

mented. "All we could do back then was line the film up on an optical printer and try to play with different exposures of light. We were trying to get rid of matte lines; there was no sense of leaving them in because they were a part of STAR WARS. Now, in the digital realm, we have such tremendous control over compositing issues, with the ability to adjust color levels, the densities of black, the size of the mattes that we use to composite."

One of the typical optical problems the Special Edition team addressed in the Hoth battlefield scenes were shots in which the snowfield back-

ground element, due to the insufficient density of the matte, seeped through into some foreground elements (in technical terms, a "transparency"). These included scenes of Luke Skywalker strapped into his snowspeeder, his cockpit window looking across the valley of snow to a distant walker—and the snow-field image seeping through the bottom of the cock-pit. "The reason they originally finaled [approved]

Left: *Millennium Falcon* enters Cloud City air space; George Hull.

Below: *Falcon* touches down on Cloud City landing platform (bird's-eye view); George Hull.

the cockpit shot is that the audience is looking up at Luke's eyes, and not the fact that there might be some snow terrain visible in the lower part of his cockpit," Carson recalled. "This is a shot in which we can just go back to the original elements and digitally recomposite them, cleaning up any transparencies."

For the cockpit shot, a foreground blue-screen element—of Luke with the walker—had to match seamlessly with the snowfield background. "The matte line is that point at which the blue-screen and background element come together, and the goal was always to make that line as imperceptible as possible," noted Tom Christopher, film editor for all

three Special Edition releases. "In opticals, the goal was not only that those elements come into register, but also to control the luminescence value so the background didn't bleed through the foreground when you lined them up [on an optical printer] and shot them onto film."

Another transparency fix was required for a shot of Luke piloting his X-wing starfighter, with Artoo-Detoo attached. An image of the craft leaving Dagobah and piloting through space had been shot as a blue-screen element, which created problems when dealing with the blue-colored parts of Luke's droid. "Because of the blue on Artoo, they originally had trouble pulling a matte without causing a transparency and having the starfield background show through," noted Julie Adrianson Neary, who provided digital rotoscoping and Artoo painting expertise on all three Special Editions. "Because they couldn't change the color, they had to paint Artoo black and then shoot the blue-screen—which has bothered George for nearly twenty years. Now we can digitally recomposite the shot and change Artoo from black back to blue."

The Special Edition team revisited Cloud City with more than digital fixes in mind. The city-in-the-sky finale of EMPIRE required enhancements that Lucas had always wanted but were impossible to achieve at the time, given the limits of having to shoot two-dimensional matte paintings with locked-off camera views. But with three-dimensional computer graphics and digital matte paintings, photorealistic buildings of Cloud City and flying craft could be constructed, using free-flying virtual camera views.

Cloud City enhancements would also include new *Millennium Falcon* fly-through shots over CG buildings (utilizing a CG *Falcon* model that had been digitally constructed for the NEW HOPE Special Edition). The team would produce a new cloud car fly-by and realistic-looking vista shots in which the curvature at the floating city edge could be perceived. They would add window views of a CG skyline, enhancing hallway scenes originally created with closed sets, and new dusk-time shots of Darth Vader walking down a platform to board his shuttle and fly up to meet his orbiting Star Destroyer (featuring new blue screen photography of a performer in a Vader suit).

"Having a CG *Falcon* and cloud cars flying through an all-CG environment is rare for ILM," noted CG animation supervisor James Tooley. "Usually we deal with a live-action background plate, where camera position and movement have already been dictated. But for our fly-through Cloud City, we're creating the camera motion of the *Falcon* and cloud cars. We can move our virtual camera however we want through the scene, with no physical constraints."

Part of the challenge was in matching the look and aesthetics of the new scenes with the existing Cloud City footage. For inspiration, the Special Edition team went back to the original production concept art of Ralph McQuarrie.

Some of McQuarrie's EMPIRE concepts hadn't made it into the final film. For the Hoth sequence the artist had provided glimpses of a perfectly preserved city mysteriously abandoned by some lost Hothian civilization, its massive spires breaking the icy crust of the surface with building foundations going down into subterranean ice caves. McQuarrie also envisioned not one Cloud City above Bespin, but floating ghost cities and land masses, as well as a creature resembling a manta ray, which flapped to and fro among the floating structures.

One of McQuarrie's original EMPIRE designs *would* make it into the Special Edition. That particular production art had visualized Cloud City buildings with windows open to the stunning vistas of the floating city, an effect too difficult to create on the film's live-action sets. Back then, to incorporate a cityscape matte painting would have limited the camera to a locked-off position, since any camera movement could instantly reveal the two-dimensional brush and oil effect. Modern digital paint systems, however, now allow artists to create photorealistic, 3-D structures that allow for perspective shifts and the creation of virtual camera moves to match any live-action camera. Thus, the Special Edition team

Storyboard sequence following cloud car travel; George Hull.

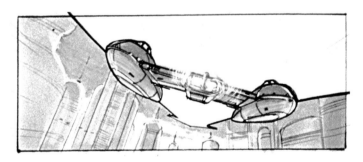

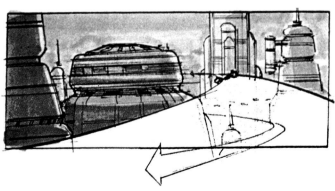

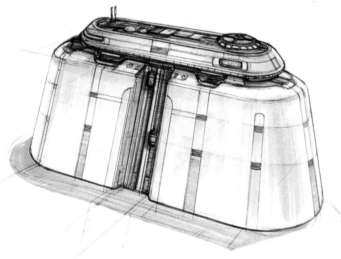

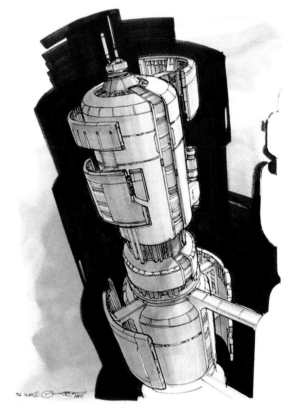

Top: Cloud City skyline and "Leia's Building" redesign by George Hull.

Above: "Leia's Building" redesign by George Hull.

Right: Empire building design; George Hull.

could now add in window with breathtaking Cloud City views.

Many of the new CG Cloud City buildings were constructed with texture maps, a computer graphics technique in which surface textures and details are applied to another image (typically a 3-D wire-frame construct). "These buildings can literally require hundreds of texture maps to get all the details, which can become a laborious process [with traditional texture mapping]," explained CG supervisor Tom Hutchinson. "We've developed an in-house [ILM] texture mapping software we call Viewpaint, an interactive process which allows an artist to paint textures directly onto a 3-D object."

And it was important that the new footage match the original film, from the look of filters on the camera lenses to the amount of film grain. "The film stock that was used in 1977 [circa the EMPIRE production] was quite different from today's film stocks, plus the negative has aged," Dave Carson explained. "In today's film stocks, the blacks are richer, the grain is smaller. It's just a problem you have when shooting new footage and intercutting it with old footage. So all these things can show up, and we have to *add* some grain [to make it match]. A lot of

Above: Cloud City view; George Hull.

Left: Thumbnail sketches for Cloud City scene; George Hull.

the problems figuring out how to make the new shots intercut with the old footage were worked out on A NEW HOPE."

Not all the Special Edition work required the cutting-edge digital technologies: New Special Edition EMPIRE shots of the fearsome wampa were produced with a scaled ice cave set and the old-fashioned man-in-a-creature suit. But the production would truly come full circle (and save on the time and expense of a digital solution) with Pacific Title's use of traditional optical printing technology to address such classic lab effects as "wipes," a visual narrative device indicating transitions of time or place and characterized by a line moving across frame as an existing image is replaced by a new image. There were thirty such shots in A NEW HOPE and forty-eight wipes in EMPIRE, such as a Hoth scene of Han

Solo waving to rescue speeders which wiped into the wampa cave interior where Luke was prisoner.

"Wipes were used in the early days of film, in things like the old Republic serials, but used less and less in the post-World War Two era," noted Tom Christopher. "I remember when I first saw STAR WARS I was shocked to see that instead of dissolves it used wipes, which hadn't been used in a long time. Sometimes when a wipe is about to happen, the grain structure of the picture changes as the wipe line comes across, which is phenomenally noticeable. Our work was to make sure there wasn't a change, bringing the quality up to a level where no one would notice them."

Pacific Title's eleven on-site printers had the

advantage of modern lenses and new fine-grain Kodak film stocks. And amazingly enough, the original visual effects elements were available to be recomposited, according to 20th Century Fox executive Ted Gagliano, who headed up the studio's involvement in the trilogy restoration. "George Lucas saved all his outtakes and optical elements, he archived everything on all three films," he explained.

"He was very smart and had some kind of foresight about doing that. He even had a Technicolor process print of the original STAR WARS in the basement of his home, which, because the colors on those prints don't fade, was an invaluable reference in getting the Special Edition to color-time exactly as it did twenty years ago."

Gagliano noted that, as they began the restora-

Above: "Closer view" of Cloud City scene; George Hull.

Right: Tilt-down of Cloud City scene; George Hull.

Opposite page, top: Concept art of Vader crossing Cloud City platform to shuttle; George Hull.

Opposite page, bottom: Thumbnail sketches of Darth Vader walking Cloud City landing platform to board his Imperial shuttle; George Hull.

tion process, they found that "the first thing people assume is to go digital, which is great because you can do anything in digital, but one of the things we shouldn't forget is that these photochemical processes have been around for a long time and there's still a lot you can do with them. That's what's been unique [about the Special Edition work], that the work has been a mixture of digital enhancements with traditional techniques used to make the wipes and other simple opticals look better than ever."

The Special Edition work would also not be complete without polishing and upgrading that important and often overlooked component of a movie production—sound. "Sound technology has changed since EMPIRE, and there are stereo and digital theater sound systems that didn't exist when the movie first came out," explained Ben Burtt, overseeing Special Edition sound editing and design, tasks he performed on the original films. "So on EMPIRE, we went back and digitally remastered the movie for best sound quality. We have a mix of the movie—dialogue, music, sound effects—and the result is many layers of sound. We can take those original layers and blend and tailor them to today's high fidelity theaters."

Burtt echoed Gagliano's tone of amazement when he noted that Lucas had held onto even all the sound elements. "It's unusual for a studio to keep hold of all the original elements," Burtt explained. "They'll usually just keep the final recording and get rid of the bits and pieces. George Lucas had the foresight and space to do it, even though over the years there was sometimes pressure to throw out these boxes of sound elements. They were stored in vari-

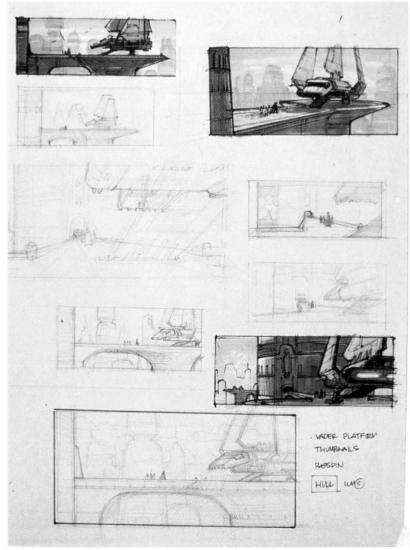

Top: Storyboard scene of Vader's shuttle leaving Bespin; George Hull.

Middle and bottom: Thumbnail sketches of Star Destroyer boarding section; George Hull.

ous warehouses in northern California and then at the Lucasfilm Archives at Skywalker Ranch."

Burtt likened the STAR WARS sound archives to a visit to the vast, mysterious warehouse glimpsed at the conclusion of RAIDERS OF THE LOST ARK. There were hundreds of boxes, each typically containing a dozen reels of magnetic sound film. On these "boxes of sound," as Burtt called them, were preserved and catalogued everything ever heard in the STAR WARS universe, including such sound effects as the beeping communications of Artoo-Detoo, the heavy-booted footfalls of Darth Vader, the crash of dueling lightsabers, even the sound of wind. While there were twelve reels of film for EMPIRE, the sound layers that would be blended together came from hundreds of thousand-foot-long sound reels. "Every little sound is part of the mosaic," Burtt concluded.

As Rick McCallum observed, although the restoration work would have been necessary for any theatrical rerelease, the Special Editions were a unique variation on the vogue for director's cuts, which typically involved adding excised scenes and radically changing the nature of the story. Instead of a massive make-over, the STAR WARS TRILOGY SPECIAL EDITION was characterized by fixes and enhancements seamlessly interwoven into the trilogy tapestry—everything Lucas wanted but couldn't achieve when he and his ILM unit were battling deadlines and pushing the limits of technology. The result, marking the twentieth anniversary of A NEW HOPE, is a trilogy for the ages.

"What I loved about the Special Editions was that George was very specific about what he wanted," noted Rick McCallum. "George always knew from memory what shots he wanted changed, what he wasn't satisfied with originally. It was, 'The dewbacks never moved, I could never get Jabba into the first film, I hated that matte shot, I hated the way the X-wing moved in that shot, I couldn't afford this or that.' At the time, you're upset, but you have to let go. That's why director's cuts come out. Making a movie is a very emotional thing."

BIOGRAPHIES

LEON BRIGGS, Special Edition restoration consultant, helped supervise the overall film restoration work on the entire trilogy. He determined the approach to cleaning and repairing the badly damaged original STAR WARS negative. Briggs left the Walt Disney Company in 1991 after an eighteen-year career as lab technician for theme park films to start his own company, LB Film Consulting. He has performed restoration magic on such classic Disney productions as SNOW WHITE and FANTASIA.

BEN BURTT, supervising sound editor and designer for the STAR WARS TRILOGY SPECIAL EDITION, headed up sound design and effects for the original releases of both the STAR WARS and Indiana Jones trilogies. His directorial projects since 1990 include first and second unit director/editor work on the YOUNG INDIANA JONES series—including directing the 1995 Young Indy cable feature ATTACK OF THE HAWKMEN—and the 1996 IMAX release SPECIAL EFFECTS.

DAVE CARSON, visual effects supervisor for EMPIRE and JEDI Special Editions, is currently the manager of ILM's visual effects supervisors group. He joined ILM to work on the original EMPIRE as a model maker and storyboard artist. His varied ILM credits include visual effects supervisor on BODY WARS (a simulator ride for Disney's EPCOT Center) in 1989; commercials directing for such spots as the Heinz Ketchup "Ants" ad (1991); CG digital artist on JURASSIC PARK (1993); and character design supervisor on CASPER (1995).

TOM CHRISTOPHER, film editor for the STAR WARS TRILOGY SPECIAL EDITION, has since 1982 specialized in postproduction film work in the San Francisco Bay Area. His Lucasfilm editorial work includes being third season editor on the YOUNG INDIANA JONES CHRONICLES, and he compiled special movie-length Young Indy episodes for video release. His first Lucasfilm project was as sound mixer and recordist on RETURN OF THE JEDI.

TED GAGLIANO headed up the Special Edition effort on the 20th Century Fox side. He has been a senior vice president for feature postproduction at 20th Century Fox since 1991 and previously served at Paramount Pictures in film and television postproduction, initially doing restoration and archival work in the studio library.

HOWARD GERSH acted as CG technical director on the STAR WARS TRILOGY SPECIAL EDITION. His EMPIRE Special Edition work concentrated on the CG Cloud City shots. He joined ILM in 1993 to add technical director expertise to such projects as FORREST GUMP (1994), RADIOLAND MURDERS (1994), and a new Universal Studios logo for theatrical trailers (1996). His work previous to ILM was at Rhythm & Hues on a variety of commercial projects, including a motion-based simulator ride for client Kia Motors (shown at the 1993 World Expo in Korea).

GEORGE HULL was visual effects art director on the EMPIRE Special Edition. Since joining ILM in 1993, Hull has worked on features in a number of capacities, including storyboard artist, concept artist, and visual effects art director. His effects art direction credits include JUMANJI (1995), MISSION: IMPOSSIBLE (1996), and the 1997 release, THE LOST WORLD. Hull's background experiences have included designing future vehicle concepts for automakers Chrysler and Ford, with an earlier stint creating simulator ride concepts and storyboards at Magic Edge Inc.

TOM HUTCHINSON, CG supervisor on the EMPIRE and JEDI Special Editions, began his ILM career with technical director duties on the 1991 Tristar release HOOK, with ensuing CG supervisory duties on the summer '96 blockbusters MISSION: IMPOSSIBLE and TWISTER. Previous to ILM he worked as senior technical director at the Metrolight effects house, contributing to 1990's TOTAL RECALL, which won a Technical Achievement Academy Award for special visual effects.

TOM KENNEDY, visual effects producer on the STAR WARS TRILOGY SPECIAL EDITION, joined ILM in 1988, bringing with him fifteen years of production and postproduction experience. His innovative ILM career includes developing and managing the company's award-winning Commercials division, as well as developing the SABRE system, ILM's real-time, interactive film and video resolution compositing suite.

RICK MCCALLUM is the producer for not only the STAR WARS TRILOGY SPECIAL EDITION and restoration, but the STAR WARS prequels in development. Rick's Lucasfilm production credits include the 1994 feature RADIOLAND MURDERS and the award-winning forty-four-episode saga of THEY YOUNG INDIANA JONES CHRONICLES television series (which garnered twenty-five Emmy nominations and won eleven Emmy awards). Previous work includes a hugely successful collaboration with the late writer Dennis Potter, bringing to the big screen Potter's PENNIES FROM HEAVEN, DREAMCHILD, BLACKEYES, TRACK 29, and THE SINGING DETECTIVE as a six-part BBC series. He has also produced David Hare's STRAPLESS and HEADING HOME, Nic Roeg's CASTAWAY, Gavin Millar's ON TIDY ENDINGS, as well as Neil Simon's I OUGHT TO BE IN PICTURES.

DENNIS MUREN has been involved from the inception of the Special Edition, beginning with the design phase for the enhanced NEW HOPE shots. A senior visual effects supervisor, Muren began his ILM career with that seminal STAR WARS unit (as visual effects second cameraman), and has helped ILM evolve from traditional to digital effects as supervisor on such breakthrough films as YOUNG SHERLOCK HOLMES (1985), THE ABYSS (1989), TERMINATOR 2 (1991), JURASSIC PARK (1993), and CASPER (1995). Along the way, he has been the recipient of eight Academy Awards for Best Achievement in Visual Effects.

JULIE ADRIANSON NEARY worked on the EMPIRE and JEDI Special Editions as a 2-D compositor. For EMPIRE she contributed digital rotoscoping and compositing work, particularly on Cloud City sequences. Hired by ILM in 1993 to work as a digital rotoscoper on FORREST GUMP, her ILM credits include DISCLOSURE (1994), CONGO (1995), and TWISTER (1996).

TOM ROSSETER was senior digital compositor on the EMPIRE and JEDI Special Editions. His ILM career has spanned traditional opticals to digital compositing. He joined ILM in 1979 to work in opticals lineup on THE EMPIRE STRIKES BACK and transitioned to the computer graphics department in 1993. His recent credits include being supervisor in charge of compositing for TWISTER (1996) and senior compositor on MISSION: IMPOSSIBLE (1996). Outside projects include the 1993 freelance restoration work on Disney's classic, SNOW WHITE.

CHAD TAYLOR, SABRE artist on the STAR WARS TRILOGY SPECIAL EDITION, joined ILM in 1993 and was involved in development of the real-time, interactive SABRE compositing system. He served as SABRE artist on such features as FORREST GUMP (1994), MISSION: IMPOSSIBLE (1996), and DRAGONHEART (1996).

JAMES TOOLEY, animation supervisor for EMPIRE and JEDI Special Editions, served as CG animator on the NEW HOPE Special Edition. He joined ILM as one of six animation supervisors on the 1995 release, CASPER. Prior to ILM, he spent five years at Walt Disney Features Animation, contributing CG artwork to such productions as ALADDIN and THE LION KING.

BRUCE VECCHITTO, digital color timer on the STAR WARS TRILOGY SPECIAL EDITION, currently serves as ILM's film group manager, which coordinates filmed elements before and after they have been scanned and manipulated in the digital realm. He joined ILM in 1985 as animation effects cameraman on YOUNG SHERLOCK HOLMES and moved into optical department lineup work for GOLDEN CHILD (1986), WHO FRAMED ROGER RABBIT? (1988), WILLOW (1988), and other films. Vecchitto contributed to the company's transition from opticals to digital while performing both traditional opticals and digital color timing on TERMINATOR 2 (1991) and DEATH BECOMES HER (1992).

RON WOODALL, viewpaint texture mapper for EMPIRE and JEDI Special Editions, concentrated on 3-D Cloud City work on EMPIRE. Prior to joining ILM in 1996, he worked as a freelance artist for EPL Productions in Orlando, Florida, and in 1995 worked in conjunction with EPL and SEGA/USA as texture mapper on a real-time video game simulator project.

RITA ZIMMERMAN, SABRE artist on the STAR WARS TRILOGY SPECIAL EDITION, has additional SABRE artist credits that include FORREST GUMP (1994), RADIOLAND MURDERS (1994), MISSION: IMPOSSIBLE (1996), and DRAGONHEART (1996). Her early ILM work includes digital artist responsibilities on JURASSIC PARK (1993); prior to ILM, she worked as a video artist and compositor at Western Images in San Francisco.

SPECIAL EDITION CREW LIST

ACKER, MICHAEL C.
AFFONSO, BARBARA
ALTROCCHI, ALEXANDRA
ANDERSON, MARK
ANDERSON, RICK
ASSMUS, CARL F.
ATAMAN, OKAN
BALCEREK, SCOTT V.
BALIEL, TERRELL L.
BARNEA, ERAN
BARR, WILLIAM
BARTLE, JOHN P.
BAUMAN, CAROL E.
BEACH, DUGAN
BEAN, RANDALL K.
BELL, WENDY
BELLBROOK, DORJE S.
BEN-JOSEPH, LEILA
BEYER, EARL W.
BIES, DONALD
BIKLIAN, ANDREA
BLAKE, NICHOLAS E.
BONNENFANT, SCOTT A.
BRACKETT, JASON A.
BRADLEY, KAREN A.
BRAY, TODD MCCUNE
BREVICK, NOEL C.
BREWER, JEFF M.
BRIMER, DANIEL
BROWN III, JAMES S.
BROWN, RONALD HARRY
BUCK, MARK C.
BUELNA, MARY C.
CALANCHINI, MICHAELA R.
CAMPANARO, JOHN N.
CAMPBELL, GEOFFREY K.
CARLSON, MEGAN I.
CARSON, DAVID
CASEY, SEAN
CHESLOFF, PETER
CLOT, ROBERT PETER
CONTE, MICHAEL J.
CONTENT, CAITLIN V.
COOPER, ANDREA L.
CORCORAN, MICHAEL J.
CREIGHTON, JULIE
DAULTON, PETER K.
DAVIS, FON H.
DELIBER, DAVID P.
DELLAROSA, LOU R.
DEMOLSKI, RICHARD S.
DEWE, BRYAN J.
DIGGORY, RONALD E.
DOHERTY, JAMES E.
DOHERTY, ROBERT M.
DONOVAN, GIOVANNI
DUNKLEY, EDWIN G.

EDWARDS, ROBERT M.
ELLIS, MICHAEL
EMMONS, ANASTASIA
ENDY, NANCY J.
FEJES, THOMAS J.
FERGUSON, AARON P.
FINLEY III, ROBERT
FIORENZA, MARK N.
FLORA, BRIAN A.
FORST, JON E.
FREDERICK, CARL
FULMER, JOSEPH S.
GAMBETTA, GEORGE
GEIDEMAN, TIMOTHY
GENUNG, FRED S.
GERNAND, BRIAN
GERSH, HOWARD P.
GREENWOOD, TIMOTHY A.
GRIFFIS, JIMMY E.
GUENIN, GRANT T.
GUTOFF, WILLIAM K.
HAGEDORN, JAMES RICHARD
HALL, NELSON KIRBY
HARB, JONATHAN S.
HAYE, AARON
HEATH, MARIANNE
HENDERSON-SHEA, JANE E.
HENDRICKSON, WENDY S.
HERON, GEOFFREY
HESKES, REBECCA A.P.
HICKS, KELA R.
HIGGINS, CLARK W.
HIRSH, EDWARD T.
HIRSH, MARGARET E.
HIRSH, MARY
HULL, GEORGE J.
HUSSEINI, MOHAMMED M.
HUSTON, PAUL
HUTCHINSON, THOMAS L.
HYMAN, GREG J.
IMAHARA, GRANT M.
ING, POLLY ANN K.
JENCKS, NANCY
JENSEN, E. ERIK
JENSVOLD, LARS P.
JERRELL, BRAD L.
JOBE, MICHAEL R.
JOHNSON, CAROLE M.
JOHNSON, KEITH L.
JOHNSON, ROBERT A.
JONES JR., W. DOUGLAS
KAO, SAMSON H.
KATZ, LOUIS A.
KENNEDY, TOM
KEY, FOREST
KING, TODD A.
KRASSER, MARSHALL R.

LASHBROOK, KIMBERLY A.
LAURANT, ALEXANDER W.
LEAPER, ANGELA T.
LEVINE, JOSHUA S.
LEW, STEWART
LEWIS, VICTORIA B.
LIM, JAMES C.
LIPNER-DROSTOVA, LISA
LIVINGSTONE, VICTORIA
LONDON, KEITH A.
LYNCH, MICHAEL
MAIDENBERG, REED A.
MANN, JULES
MARKELL, ALYSON
MARKS, JOSHUA
MARSHALL, TIA L.
MARTIN, DAWN E.
MARTINEK, THOMAS W.
MASSON, TERRENCE O.
MATHER, WILLIAM K.
MATHESON, DAWN D.
MCCULLOCH, MARY B.
MCGOVERN, MICHAEL JOSEPH
MCNAMARA, SCOTT THOMAS
MCPARTLAND, LADD
MEEKER, GARRICK B.
MEEKS, NICHOLAS A.
METTEN, JOSEPH P.
MICHKA, NEIL D.
MILLER, CHRISTOPHER R.
MILLER, RICHARD
MITCHELL, TODD A.
MOLATORE, TERRY A.
MONGOVAN, JOHN
MONTERROSA, MELISSA
MOORE, MARK
MORGAN, TIMOTHY J.
MORSE, JEFFREY R.
MORTON, WENDY L.
MOYNIHAN, KENNETH W.
MUREN, DENNIS
MURPHY, DAVID M.
NEARY, JULIE ADRIANSON
NELSON, DAN MARK
NONA, JENNIFER
O'HARE, HARRY J.
OLAGUE, MICHAEL R.
OLSON, JEFFREY E.
ORFALI, KHATSHO
ORTENBERG, JASON
OTTENBERG, RANDY
OWEN, DAVID J.
OZAROW, BETH H.
PARRISH, DAVID A.
PASQUARELLO, EDWARD M.
PELKEY, BILL
PETERSON, ALAN H.

PINES, JOSHUA
PIPER, VANCE R.
PITONE, ANTHONY
POLLAND, ANNE
PRECIADO, JUAN A.
RAMOS, RICARDO
REED, CHRISTOPHER A.
RITTS, SANDY
ROSSETER, THOMAS
ROTHBART, JONATHAN
RYAN, JOSEPH
SAENZ, PATRICE D.
SCHMIDT, HEIDI
SEFLOVA, JARMILA
SERAFINI, MARY EGAN
SHUMAKER, DANIEL
SIEGEL, MARK
SMITH, DOUGLAS E.
SMITH, DOUGLAS J.
SMITH, KENNETH
SMITH, SANDRA LISA
SORBO, BRIAN
SPAH, RICHARD
STANTON, BROOKE A.
STARR, CHRISTA S.
STILLMAN, CHRISTOPHER L.
TAN, LAWRENCE
TANAKA, DAVID H.
TAYLOR, CHAD M.
THEREN, PAUL
THOMPSON, DEREK
TODD, IRMA E.
TOOLEY, JAMES R.
TURKO, JENNY-KING
TURNER, PATRICK ALAN
UESUGI, YUSEI
UHLIG, HANS H.
VAN EPS, MICHAEL D.
VECCHITTO, BRUCE
VOEGELS, ERIC D.
WAGNER, DANIEL J.
WALLACE, KEVIN C.
WALLIN, MATTHEW
WALTON, STEVEN J.
WANK, JONATHAN S.
WASHBURN, SHANE L.
WEED, HAROLD
WEI, LI-HSIEN
WHISNANT, JOHN DAVID
WILEY, CHARLES H.
WOODALL, RONALD L.
WOODBRIDGE, JULIE A.
ZABIT, HEIDI J.
ZIMMERMAN, RITA E.